John Stuart Blackie

Lyrical Poems

John Stuart Blackie

Lyrical Poems

ISBN/EAN: 9783744788151

Printed in Europe, USA, Canada, Australia, Japan

Cover: Foto ©Andreas Hilbeck / pixelio.de

More available books at **www.hansebooks.com**

LYRICAL POEMS.

BY

JOHN STUART BLACKIE,

PROFESSOR OF GREEK IN THE UNIVERSITY OF EDINBURGH.

EDINBURGH: SUTHERLAND AND KNOX.

LONDON: SIMPKIN, MARSHALL, & CO.

MDCCCLX.

MURRAY AND GIBB, PRINTERS, EDINBURGH.

TO

THE REV. THOMAS GUTHRIE, D.D.,

A FAITHFUL PASTOR,

AN ACTIVE PHILANTHROPIST,

A LARGE-HEARTED MAN,

AND

A POET AMONG PREACHERS,

These Poems

ARE DEDICATED

BY

HIS SINCERE FRIEND,

THE AUTHOR.

Wie nimmt ein leidenschaftlich Stammeln
    Geschrieben sich so seltsam aus !
    Nun soll ich gar von Haus zu Haus
Die losen Blaetter alle sammeln.

Was eine lange weite Strecke
    Im Leben von einander stand,
    Das kommt nun unter Einer Decke
Dem guten Leser in die Hand.

Doch schaeme dich nicht der Gebrechen,
    Vollende schnell das kleine Buch ;
    Die Welt ist voller Widerspruch,
Und sollte sich 's nicht widersprechen ?

GOETHE.

CONTENTS.

BOOK I.—CLIO.

BOOK II.—POLYHYMNIA.

BOOK III.—ERATO.

BOOK IV.—EUTERPE.

CONTENTS.

BOOK V.—CAMENA.

BOOK I.

CLIO.

The solemn League and Covenant
  Cost Scotland blood, cost Scotland tears !
But Faith sealed Freedom's sacred cause ;
  If thou'rt a slave indulge thy sneers.—BURNS.

PATRICK HAMILTON.[1]

In St Andrew's grey-towered city
   Once was done a deed unholy,
When the harsh and haughty churchman
   Crushed the martyr meek and lowly.
Young was he, and gentle-thoughted,
   Blood of kings flowed in his veins ;
But with manly mild endurance
   Stout he bore the fiery pains.
And he gave his life a priceless
   Ransom, to make Scotland free,
By the faith which scorns the faggot,
   Bloody priest of Rome, from thee.
Hoar St Andrews, thou didst witness,
   When the dark-stoled priestly crew
Came swift trooping, where the trumpet
   Of the far-feared Beaton blew.

Thou didst see the mitred council
    Sit, and, with a ghastly prayer,
Pray the God who loves his creatures
    To make foulest murder fair
With holy names; and thou didst hear it
    When, instead of reasons true,
Age gave grace to doting dogma,
    Truth was damned because 'twas new.
And for burning words heart-kindling,
    Soulless creeds were grimly read
From books, that with a monstrous learning
    Slaved the living to the dead.
They with sounding pomp disputed,
    Meekly he, and calmly wise;
They with curious deft manœuvre,
    He with short plain text replies.
Forth then went that calm refuter,
    While they muttered spiteful wrath,
And the mob, with senseless clamour,
    Hooted round his guiltless path.
To the place of doom they led him,
    In his hand the holiest book;
Bright the noon-day sun was shining,
    Brighter shone the martyr's look.

To the bloody stake they bound him
  With strong bonds, who needed none :
Freely to the fiery torture
  Marched the noble Hamilton.
Blessings for their hateful curses
  He returned ; his voice implored
Pardon to his stone-eyed murderers,
  While the blazing billet roared.
God was with him in his anguish,
  Jesus gave him strength divine;
He, like Stephen, saw the glory
  Through the wreathed darkness shine.
And a glorious light behind him
  Shone—and shines—whose death made free
Scotland, spite of fire and faggot,
  Bloody priest of Rome, from thee !
And the towers of grey St Andrews,
  By the roaring German wave,
While we name his name, shall teach us
  To be gentle, true, and brave.

THE TWO MEEK MARGARETS.[2]

It fell on a day in the blooming month of May,
   When the trees were greenly growing,
That a captain grim went down to the brim
   O' the sea, when the tide was flowing.

Twa maidens he led, that captain grim,
   Wi' his red-coat loons behind him,
Twa meek-faced maids, and he sware that he
   In the salt sea-swell should bind them.

And a' the burghers o' Wigton town
   Came down, full sad and cheerless,
To see that ruthless captain drown
   These maidens meek, but fearless.

O what had they done, these maidens meek,
  What crime all crimes excelling,
That they should be staked on the ribbed sea-sand,
  And drowned, where the tide was swelling?

O wae's me, wae! but the truth I maun say!
  Their crime was the crime of believing
Not man, but God, when the last false Stuart
  His Popish plot was weaving.

O spare them! spare them! thou captain grim!
  No! no!—to a stake he hath bound them,
Where the floods as they flow, and the waves as
    they grow,
  Shall soon be deepening round them.

The one had threescore years and three;
  Far out on the sand they bound her,
Where the first dark flow of the waves as they grow
  Is quickly swirling round her.

The other was a maiden fresh and fair;
  More near to the land they bound her,
That she might see by slow degree
  The grim waves creeping round her.

O captain, spare that maiden grey,
    She's deep in the deepening water!
No! no!—she's lifted her hands to pray,
    And the choking billow caught her!

See, see, young maid, cried the captain grim,
    The wave shall soon ride o'er thee!
She's swamped in the brine whose sin was like thine;
    See that same fate before thee!

I see the Christ who hung on a tree
    When His life for sins He offered;
In one of His members, even He
    With that meek maid hath suffered.

O captain, save that meek young maid;
    She's a loyal farmer's daughter!
Well, well! let her swear to good King James,
    And I'll hale her out from the water!

I will not swear to Popish James,
    But I pray for the head of the nation,
That he and all, both great and small,
    May know God's great salvation!

She spoke; and lifted her hands to pray,
    And felt the greedy water,
Deep and more deep, around her creep,
    Till the choking billow caught her!

O Wigton, Wigton! I'm wae to sing
    The truth o' this waesome story;
But God will sinners to judgment bring,
    And His saints shall reign in glory.

ELEGY ON THE DEATH OF JAMES RENWICK.[3]

WEEP, Scotland, weep!   Thy hills are sad to-day,
   But not with mist or rack that skirs the sky.
The violent rule ; the godless man holds sway ;
   The young, the pure, the innocent must die !
Weep, Scotland, weep ! thy moors are sad to-day,
   Thy plaided people walk with tearful eye.
For why?   He dies upon a gallows-tree
Who boldly blew God's trump for Freedom and for
   thee !

'Tis a known tale ; it hath been so of old,
   And will be so again ; yet must we weep !
High on red thrones the blushless and the bold
   Hold state ; the meek are bound in dungeons
     deep.
Wolves watch the pen ; the lion robs the fold,
   While on soft down the hireling shepherds sleep.

God's holy church becomes a mart, where lies
Pass free from knave to fool, but Christ's true
    prophet dies.

A youth was Renwick, gentle, fair, and fine ;
    In aspect meek, but firm as rock in soul ;
By pious parents nursed, and holy line,
    To steer by truth, as seamen by the pole.
In Holland's learned halls the word divine
    He read, which to proclaim he made the whole
Theme of his life ; then back to Scotland came,
At danger's call, to preach in blessed Jesus' name.

They watched his coming, and the coast with spies
    Planted to trap him ; but he 'scaped their snare.
To the brown hills and glens of Kyle he hies,
    And with a stedfast few finds refuge there.
On the black bogs, and 'neath the inclement skies,
    In rocky caves, on mist-wreathed mountains bare,
The youthful prophet voiced God's tidings good,
As free as Baptist John by Jordan's sacred flood.

Fierce fumed the ruthless king. By statute law,
    To sing God's praise upon a purple hill

Was treason.   Courtly slaves with envy saw
    One unbought soul assert a manly will,
And with his own hands from those fountains draw,
    Which sophists troubled with pretentious skill
To make them clearer; as if God's own plan
For fining human dross must beg a stamp from
    man!

Wide o'er the moors now tramp the red dragoons,
    To hunt God's plaided saints from every nook;
And from a court of bravoes and poltroons
    Goes forth the law which takes the blessed book
From the free shepherds' hands, that hireling loons
    May spell it to a sense that kings may brook.
Far raged o'er heath and hill the despot's sword,
But faithful Renwick preached, and owned no human
    lord.

Bold as when Peter in the temple stood
    With John, and, at the gate called Beautiful,
Healed the lame man, and stirred the spiteful mood
    Of priest and high-priest, holding haughty rule;
Witless! who weened that God's apostles should
    With human law and lawyers go to school:

So boldly Renwick stood; and, undismayed,
With firm unfaltering faith, God and not man obeyed.

And faithful people loved him. From green Ayr,
   Nithsdale, Glencairn, Sanquhar, and founts of
     Ken,
Free pilgrim feet o'er perilous pathways fare,
   To hear young Renwick preach in treeless glen ;
And mothers bring their new-born babes, to bear
   Baptismal blessings from his touch ; and when
Fearless he flings the glowing word abroad,
Full many a noble soul is winged with fire from God.

Yet must he die ! The fangs of Law are keen ;
   False Law, the smooth pretender of the Right,
That still to knaves a sharp-edged tool hath been,
   To give a fair name to usurping Might !
By Law round noble Hamilton, I ween,
   The faggot blazed to feed proud Beaton's spite ;
And now when Scotland's best, to please the Pope
And Romish James, must die—'tis Law that knots
   the rope !

Let loose your hounds, cold-blooded lawyers ! pay
   The knave to trap the saint ! Your work is done.

Young Renwick falls, to venal spies a prey,
　　And lawless Law kills Scotland's purest son.
The grey Grassmarket heard him preach to-day,
　　On the red scaffold's floor.　His race is run.
Now kings and priests, with brave light-hearted joy,
May drain　their　cups,　nor　fear　that　bold　truth-
　　speaking boy !

Weep ! Scotland, weep ! but only for a day ;
　　Frail stands the throne, whose props are glued
　　　　with gore ;
For a short hour the godless man holds sway,
　　And Justice whets her knife at Murder's door.
Weep, Scotland ! but let noble Pride this day
　　Beam　through thine eye with sorrow streaming
　　　　o'er ;
For why ?—Thy Renwick's dead, whose noble crime
Gave Freedom's trumpet breath, an hour before the
　　time !

LINES WRITTEN IN WIGTON CHURCHYARD.[1]

BRAVE brother Scot, who in that name
Nursest the pride that worth may claim,
Come here ; and let no Southron blame
    Thy free-shed sorrow
O'er martyrs' graves, whence our true fame
    And strength we borrow!

No pillared pomp enroofs the dead,
Who for their country's freedom bled ;
No bannered hatchments overspread
    These grave-stones hoary ;
But tears with sacred virtue shed
    Keep green their glory.

Look on those granite hills around,
Strong, but more strong Scotch hearts were
        found,
When to the cruel stake were bound
        Stout Galloway's daughters,
And for dear Christ, his love, were drowned
        In briny waters.

Meek womanhood, how strong art thou,
When truth thee binds and holy vow!
For thee no trumpet blows, I trow,
        Nor chariot rattles;
But Love, throned on thy constant brow,
        Wins blameless battles.

A curse dwell with your evil name,
Strachan and Winram, Grierson, Graham!
On hangman's hest unblest ye came
        To Wigton waters,
And staked i' the swelling tide—O shame!
        Her high-souled daughters!

Torn from sweet life, so young, so good,
And cast to the devouring flood,

For that your independent mood
        The Pope's crowned minion
Spurned, when uncalled he dared intrude
        On Christ's dominion !

Weep !—it is well to weep; for why ?
Not for their sakes who so did die,
But, 'fore the righteous God on high,
        To find expression,
For burning hate of tyranny,
        And damned oppression !

Such tears make men.   Let foplings sigh
For pomp of dainty prelacy ;
But, while we read with streaming eye
        These grave-stones hoary,
We'll train stout hearts to live and die
        For Christ, His glory.

WIGTON 1859.

A SONG OF CARDINAL BEATON.[5]

The Cardinal slept in St Andrew's tower,
'Twixt the morning grey, and the midnight hour,
And he dreamt of his leman, a lady fine,
Who mingled sweet phrase with the sparkling wine,
Whispering, whispering, daintily so—
" Cardinal Beaton to Rome shall go,
And wear the tiara, my priestly joe!"
The Cardinal heard her sweet lips' flow,

But he did not hear the chorus wild,
That moaned through the night, with words not
    mild,
Saying, Down to hell!—for so 'tis right—
With Cardinal Beaton, the Pope's proud knight,
Who murdered Wishart, the godly wight!
   Down—down—down—to hell
    With the Pope and Cardinal Beaton!

The Cardinal slept in his strong sea-tower,
When the sun rose bright in the morning hour,

And he dreamt no more of his lady fine,
But he heard strange sounds through the fumes of his
  wine.
He heard a clatter, he heard a fall,
He heard a clink, and an angry call,
He heard a shout that rent the air,
And he heard the tramp of a foot on the stair :
  But he did not hear the words of Fate,
  Deep-muttered from hell's black yawning
    gate,
  Saying, *Down to hell!—for so 'tis right—*
  With Cardinal Beaton, whose haughty spite
  Murdered Wishart, the godly wight!
   Down—down—down—to hell
   With the Pope and Cardinal Beaton!

The Cardinal rose ; from the window he cried,
Who's there ?—They've ta'en thy palace of pride !
He ran to the postern-gate ; but, lo !
It was bolted and barred, and watched by the foe !
Behind his chamber-door he made
With chests and benches a barricade ;
But with smoking coals and wreathed flame
They stormed the door,—and in they came !

Ah ! then he heard, but he heard too late,
The grim death-chant of the vengeful Fate,
Saying, *Down to hell!—for so 'tis right—*
With blood-stained Beaton, whose haughty spite
Murdered Wishart, the godly wight !
     Down—down—down—to hell
     With the Pope and Cardinal Beaton !

The Cardinal staggered, and back in his chair
He fell.   They held their daggers bare.
O spare me ! spare my life !   Shall I,
A priest, be butchered ?—fie ! fie ! fie !
Full well we know that thou art a priest,
A murderer foul, and a lecherous beast !
They stabbed him once, and they stabbed him twice,
And his soul went out, when they stabbed him thrice :
     And he heard in his ears, as in darkness he fell,
     The Chorus of judgment with rending yell,
     Saying, Blood for blood ! for so 'tis right,
     Thou blood-stained Beaton, whose hand did smite
     The gentle Wishart, the godly wight !
        Blood cries for blood, in the nethermost hell,
        With the Pope and Cardinal Beaton !

MAY 1859.

WALTER MYLN.[6]

Non nostra impietas, aut actæ crimina vitæ
Armarunt hostes in mea fata truces,
Sola fides Christi, sacris signata libellis,
Quæ vitæ causa est, est mihi causa necis.
—Epitaph on Myln by PATRICK ADAMSON,
Archbishop of St Andrews.

ONE breezy day, when all the sea was white
With hoary crests, that rose upon the brine,
Like ruffled plumes upon a fretted bird,
Behind St Andrew's old grey towers I stood,
And paced with pensive foot the high-raised walk,
Which northward looks across the bay, to where
The far red headland, eastward stretching, flouts

The keen dry blast.   As I was musing there
Of ancient times and new, bishops and priests,
Martyrs and saints, and sage philosophers,
And bright-eyed dames, who shine in learning's halls,
Like gay birds flitting through a dusky grove;
There comes before my path a little man,
Smooth and close shaven, very trig and smug,
And well-appointed, not a speck of dust
On all his long black coat, which down beneath
His slender hams, near to his ankle fell;
A snow-white neckcloth with a dainty tie
Embraced his neck, whose skin was fair and fine
As any damsel's :—with a simpering lisp
He spake, and asked me—Pray, Sir, can you tell
What man was Walter Myln?   I, like a Scot,
Replied—Why ask you that?   I read, quoth he,
That name upon the obelisk, which stands
High-perched above the benty golfing ground,
And, being here a stranger, fain would know
What names you honour in this Northern land;
Our saints in Oxford have a larger fame,
And sound through time, their own interpreter.
O yes ! I said, you Southern Square-caps know
As much of Scotland, as a fly that's bred

In a grocer's sugar-cask may comprehend
Of honeyed heather and of mountain bees.
Our glens, you deem, are pleasant hunting-ground
For London brewers and ducal debauchees,
And our fair lochs and mountains a rare show
To salve blear eyes, sick with a six months' view
Of peevish faces in a hot saloon!
But, since your question hints some stray regard
For Scottish worthies, and the sacred blood
That glued the stones of our stout Scottish Kirk,
I'll tell you what I know,—though, in good sooth,
Not much is known of Myln, and even that little
By flippant wits is mostly overskipped,
Whose eye is all for courts and cavaliers,
Crowns, mitres, coronets, and gaudy crests,
Stars, crosses, ribbons, painted heraldries,
The pomp and flare of life; but quiet worth
In strong-souled martyr, or meek-suffering saint,
Like some fair flower in hollow glen remote,
Finds not their wanton eye.   So said, I drew
A circle round my thoughts, and them adjured
To do their master's will; and to the smug,
Smooth-lipped Oxonian thus my tale began :

Myln, like most men, in those unbookish days,
Who had no taste for arms, was bred to the church ;
And as our Scotland lies remote, a small
Creek in the wide sea of the world, where tides
Are latest felt, he sailed abroad, and spread
The germing blossoms of his youthful thought,
To burst before the doctors of Almayne,
Most learned and subtle.   There, belike, his ear
Caught the first stirrings of the God-sent gale,
Which, blown tempestuous from the shrilling trump
Of a poor Saxon monk, smote branchy Rome
With dwindling fear, and from the roots uptore
Her pride o'er half the world.   Thence he returned,
Stirred by new thoughts, and thrilled by poignant
    doubts,
To his dear Scotland, where for many years
The daily offices of the church he used,
And plied the faithful round of priestly service,
In Lunan's sandy bay.   The outward man
Long time was calm ; but still the ferment worked
Of the new doctrine, which the times had imped
Into his budding soul, and his heart swayed
With strange discomfort ; till his ripened thoughts
Grew larger than his place, and he must burst

Old bonds of life.   Then, like an embryo bird,
One day—he knew not how, but God that morn
Had pricked his soul—he burst his shelly case,
Claimed his due portion in a larger life,
And stood a freeman in a land of slaves.
Like as a man, who, in some dusty nook
Of an old lumber-room, amid a heap
Of yellowed papers, lavishly bescrawled
With silly records of ephemeral loves,
And trivial sorrows, suddenly hath spied
A parchment signed and sealed, whose stamp revives
Lost claims, his rusted right refurbishes,
And makes him lord of long mislorded roods;
Into new life he starts, surveys the world
With bolder scope, breathes a more ample breath,
And stands a peer, who late had crouched a slave:
Even so this simple priest, before the power
Of misvouched creeds and a mistutored church,
Stood, with the new-found Bible in his hand,
Which God's own finger wrote.—Forthwith he went,
And preached the precious truth he knew to all,
As free as he had found it; but not all
Would gladly hear it.   Few had wit to know;
And of these few, the fewest with strong nerve

Could bear the radiant truth, but dubious lived,
Fearing the dark, and blinking at the day.
Who flings broad truth into a falsèd age
Must count his foes by thousands, and his friends
By units.   So, indeed, the priesthood raised
About poor Myln a clattering hue and cry,
As he were known a thief, and rent the ears
O' the fever'd time with fretful bickerment;
And him at length in Dysart town—a place
More bruited then than now—they rudely seized,
And to St Andrew's hoary castle haled,
And barred him in yon tower beside the sea,
Whose dungeon yet smelt rank with innocent blood
Of Wishart, and the noble Hamilton.
There first with baits of fleshly lure they tipped
Their sensual hooks, and promised him a stall
In rich Dunfermline's abbey, there to live
In fatted comfort, and to slide at ease
Into a cushioned grave.   But not such man
Such straw might tickle.   So, from prison dragged,
Before the assembly of the priests he stood,
Even in the pulpit of the Bishop's church
Impeached of heresy; and fearless there
With meek aspect fronted the proud array

Of priests and bishops, priors, provosts, all
The knighthood of the Pope, with motley troops
Of friars, black, and white, and grey, as thick
As flies, that on a sweltering summer day
Have scented carrion in a clover field—
Even in the great church metropolitan
He in the pulpit stood, a weak old man,
But firm, with face serene, and shaded soft
With the mild dignity of fourscore years,
To answer for his faith.   They on a bench
Sate lofty-throned, and with full lofty looks
Surveyed the people, or with face composed
To meek devotion, while high-vaulting pride
Housed in their hearts; some only fat and dull,
And gross with swinish habitude of soul,
That made them grunt, when any cleanly foot
Intruded on their sty.   Before such court
Sworn in God's name, and to their murtherous work
Invoking Father, Son, and Holy Ghost,
Stood Walter Myln.   How they accused him, what
The counts of his offending, you may read
In Foxe's book of gospel witnesses;
How he had dared, as any creature dares,
To find a mate, and mingle with his like;

How he had said that bread was bread, not flesh,
And wine plain wine, not very blood of God ;
How he declared that bishops were no bishops,
Who marketed in holy things, to feed
Not Christ's dear flock, but their own pride ; and how
From land to land he pilgrimed, not to kiss
The bones of maundering monks, and patter prayers
To swart-faced Maries prink'd with trumperies,
But with free power to preach the eternal law
Of truth and love, and righteousness to men !
All this he patient heard, and inly wept
To think that reasoning men should reason use,
To lift flat nonsense into attitudes
Of lofty sense, strutting on learnèd stilts,
And weaving curious webs of twisted phrase,
Not to reveal, but to conceal the truth.
Then, when their talk was done, he rose, and flung
Their trivial charges from his swelling soul,
Like straw before the wind ; for God inspired
The old man's heart with breath of truth, that he,
His hot youth boiling in his aged breast,
Made nave and choir to ring and sound again,
So stoutly he protested.   Wilt thou recant ?
Quoth Oliphant—so hight the questioning clerk—

If not, the fire is waiting ; thou shalt die.

Then calmly thus the old man spake : I STAND

ACCUSED OF LIFE. I KNOW THAT I MUST DIE,

SOME DAY NOT DISTANT. THEREFORE WHAT YOU

    DO,

DO QUICKLY. PROVE ME. I WILL NOT RECANT

GOD'S TRUTH ; FOR I AM CORN ; I AM NO CHAFF.

NEITHER WITH WIND SHALL I BE BLOWN AWAY,

NOR BURST BY FLAIL ; BUT I WILL BOTH ABIDE.

And so he made his brave confession, words

Worth libraries of tinkling rhetoric,

Words that made Scotland free, and eftsoons drave

The tyrannous Pope and all his company

Of mitred hirelings from our ransomed land.

But first he gave, like Socrates, his life

To pledge his words ; and so with gore they shent

His silvery locks, and for a winding-sheet

Swathed him in flaming pitch ; yet not without

Deep grudge of honest men. The people's heart

Was sick of blood, nor wished the old man dead.

The minions of the priesthood were constrained—

For none would lend a rope—to cut the cords

Of their own tents, to bind him to the stake ;

Where being fixed, he stood like one entranced

With holy rapture and serene discourse.
Yet not with dumb submission died; once more,
While life remained, and the keen-crackling blaze,
Choked not his utterance, his free voice he raised
For truth and right, and God and Christ.   And all
The people's hearts were moved; and many wept—
Though tears were perilous then—and inly curst
The priestly bonds they had no strength to break.

And so my tale was told.   I saw my smooth
Oxonian friend had only half a mind
To hear my story out; for these Square-caps
Give their free right hand to the Pope, to us
With grudging grace their left; but I was pleased
To blurt a dash of broad-cast Scottish truth,
Against his lisping lips.   Well, well! he says,
You Scotsmen are a pertinacious brood,
And have that harsh-grained stuff in you, which makes
Bigots and martyrs, democrats and bores;
Fitly you wear the thistle in your cap,
As in your grim theology!   I laughed.
O we're not all so fierce!   God knows, you'll find
Well-combed and smooth-licked gentlemen enough
In our saloons, who will rejoice with you,

To sneer at massive Calvin's close-wedged creed,
Who think John Knox a boor, who dared to speak
Truth to a pretty face topped with a crown;
Who hold that preachers should, like peers, avouch
Their right to preach, by links of pedigree
From Paul or Peter; whom a fervid prayer,
Or a bold word turns to nice squeamishness;
Who sigh for liturgies and surplices,
And all the frippery of your silken church!
Fear not!—the memory of our iron times
Frets the fine nerves of this too gentle age.
Our very streets are prankt with Prelacy;
The squares of breezy Edinburgh show
Statues to perjured princes, men who lived
Chief captains of a swinish court, and died
With rotten souls embalmed in Popery.
Proud monuments are piled to eternise
Lawyers with supple conscience and glib tongue,
And frizzled kings, with never a deeper thought
Than their rolled waistcoats—but you'll beat in vain
Those streets, to find one stone to memorise
Dauntless John Knox, or faithful Walter Myln.

So my Scotch bile I vented; and our ways

We parted : he across the golfing ground,
Whence blew the railway's screeching whistle ; I
To hold discourse with sage philosophers
Of knowing and of being, and to feed
Mine eyes with pleasant play of kindly looks
From bright-eyed dames, who shine in learning's halls,
Like gay birds flitting through a dusky grove.

                                   AUGUST 1859.

SUNDAY AT ETTRICK KIRK.[1]

<div style="text-align:center">~~~~~~~~~</div>

Who has not heard of Boston?   I,
  When I was young, and lived on books,
Upon his grave theology,
  With earnest heart and sober looks,

Would pore long hours, while lighter youths
  Drew out the sleepy morn ; nor now
Hold cheap that form of close-linked truths,
  Which I did meekly then allow

For sole true gospel.   Flippant wits
  Sneer, and will sneer ; but Calvin's plan
With Scottish temper nicely fits,
  To form the iron-purposed man,

c

Who fights for God, when God commands,
    Fearing nor frowns, nor smiles, nor tears
Of man, and to light Pleasure's bands
    Who sternly stops his practised ears.

So may it be !—soft Southern airs
    Belike may breed soft faiths ; but, while
The thistle in his cap he wears,
    For Calvin's creed on Scottish soil

No Scotsman blush !—In Ettrick glen
    I'll pray this day with faith sincere,
And worship with the plaided men,
    Who Boston's godly fame revere.

What though no gilded domes uprise,
    Quaint arch, and curious-pillared tower,
No painted lights to charm the eyes ;
    Here men both preach and pray with power.

What though no organ's skilful chimes
    Roll through long aisle or vaulted hall,
The broad-browed shepherd, with grave rhymes
    From lusty heart on God doth call.

No nice luxurious faith is here ;
   No cushioned creed for ladies fine ;
No silken priest, in dainty ear
   Smoothly to lisp the sleepy line.

Here let me worship.   Mighty God !
   Whom our firm Fathers knew with fear,
Make thou my heart the chaste abode
   Of faith, strong, manly, and severe !

JOHN·FRAZER.[a]

~~~~~~~~~~~

John Frazer was a pious man,
  Who dwelt in lone Dalquhairn,
Where huge hills feed the founts of Ken,
  'Twixt Sanquhar and Carsphairn.

King Charles, he was a despot fell;
  With harlots and buffoons
He filled his court, and scoured the hills
  With troopers and dragoons.

For he hated all the godly men,
  When, free on heather braes,
Their hearts would brim with an holy hymn
  To their great Maker's praise.
~~~~~~~~~~~

And he hated good John Frazer,
    And he bade his troopers ride
Up dale and dell, by crag and fell,
    And snow-wreathed mountain side.

One night in bleak December,
    When the snow was drifting down,
John Frazer sate by his ingle-side
    With his good wife Marion.

And they spake, as godly folk will speak,
    O' the kirk, and the kirk's concerns,
Of hair-breadth 'scapes in thousand shapes,
    And they spake o' their bonnie bairns.

Tramp, tramp !—Who's there?—'Tis they, O Heaven !
    The Devil's own errand loons !
They've lifted the latch, and there they stand,
    Six striding stark dragoons !

Too late, too late, thou crop-eared Whig !
    Too late to turn and flee !
To-morrow thou'lt dance thy latest jig,
    High on a gallows-tree !

They bound his arms and legs with thongs,
    As hard as they were able:
Then took him where their horses stood,
    And locked him in the stable.

Then back to the house they came, and bade
    The sorrowful gudewife pour
The stout brown ale—for well they knew
    She kept a goodly store.

The gudewife was a prudent dame:
    The stout brown ale brought she;
They filled and quaffed, and quaffed and filled,
    And talked with boisterous glee.

And many a ribald song they sang,
    And told in jeering strain
How God's dear saints were seized and bound,
    And hounded o'er the main.

And many an ugly oath they swore,
    That made the gudewife turn pale;
But she smoothed her face with a decent grace,
    And still she poured the ale.

And still they drank, and still they sang,
  And still they cursed and swore :
The clock struck twelve ! the clock struck one !
  And still they cried for more.

The gudewife was a prudent dame,
  She broached her ripest store :
The clock struck two ! the clock struck three !
  And still the gudewife did pour.

Then up and spake the first dragoon ;
  Now mount and grip the reins, boys !
It suits not well that a bold dragoon
  Should drink away his brains, boys !

Then up they rose, and, with an oath,
  Went reeling to the stable ;
Their steeds bestrode, and off they rode
  As fast as they were able.

With lamp in hand the gudewife rose
  And to the stable ran,
And looked, and looked, till in a nook
  She found her own gudeman !

"Now God be praised !—he's fresh and hale !
    A mighty work this day
The Lord hath done !—the stout brown ale
    Hath stol'n their wits away."

Eftsoons she brought a huge sharp knife,
    And cut the thongs in tway ;
"Now run, gudeman, and save thy life !
    They'll be back by break o' day !"

And off he ran, like a practised man—
    For oft for his life ran he—
And lurked in the hills, till God cast down
    King Charles and his company.

And lived to tell, when over the wave
    Went James with his Popish loons,
How God by stout brown ale did save
    His life from the drunk dragoons.

A SONG OF SCOTTISH HEROES.

(TUNE—*The Garb of Old Gaul.*)

I'LL sing you a song, if you'll hear me like men,
Of the land of the mountain, the rock, and the glen,
And the heroes who bled for the old Scottish cause,
When the Southron insulted our kirk and our laws ;
  For we'll make a stand for Scotland yet, the
    Wallace and the Bruce,
  Though frosty wits may sneer at home, and
    Cockneys pour abuse !
  With the fire of Robert Burns, and the faith of
    stout John Knox,
  We'll be more than a match for the smooth
    English folks !

In the moor and the mountain, the strath, and the
  glen,
Every rock tells a tale of the brave Scottish men,

Of the high-hearted martyrs, who made the king pause,
When he swindled our freedom, and tramped on our
    laws.
       For we'll make, etc.

The king lost his head—fools may whimper and whine;
But he lost it, believe me, by judgment divine,
When he came, a crowned traitor, to pick wicked
    flaws
In the Covenant, the bond of our old Scottish cause.
       For we'll make, etc.

Our kings were the godly, the grey-plaided men,
Who preached on the mountains, and prayed in the
    glen,
When the weak shuffling Charles, who swore false to
    the cause,
Sent his troopers to tramp on the old Scottish laws !
       For we'll make, etc.

There are prigs who will sneer, there are snobs who
    will laugh,
There are fools who will frown, when this bumper I
    quaff;

But here's to the men, who, like grey granite wa's,
Stood firm, when the Stuart down trampled our laws.
For we'll make, etc.

They bled on the bleak moor, they hung on a tree,
They pined in black dungeons, were drowned in the
    sea ;
But their blood was the cement that soldered our
    laws,
When they bled for their faith in the old Scottish
    cause.
For we'll make, etc.

Then here's to the men, who made monarchs to quail,
Cargill and Cameron, Guthrie, M'Kail ;
Their fame shall be sounded with deathless applause,
Who fought, bled, and died for our kirk and our laws !
For we'll make, etc.

THE MERRY BALLAD OF STOCK GEILL.[10]

GOOD lords and ladies, who refuse to bend before a
    log,
I'll tell you of a merry gest, that gave the Pope a shog;
A gest that chanced in Embro' town, and in the
    High Street old,
Where Willock taught, and stout John Knox, that
    faithful preacher bold.
    Sing hey Stock Geill ! and ho Stock Geill ! the
        tale I tell is true ;
    We dashed his bones against the stones, and his
        stump in flinders flew !

'Twas the first day of September, and the priests were
    all agog,
All through the town, with pomp to bear the newly-
    painted log ;

For the old Stock Geill, the silly god, was in the
    North Loch drowned,
And they have beaten about about, till a new one
    they have found.
    Sing hey Stock Geill! and ho Stock Geill! the
        old god and the new!
    We dashed his bones against the stones, and his
        stump in flinders flew!

There goes a stir through all the streets, a buzz
    through all the town;
With banners, flags, and crosses they are walking up
    and down;
The Regent queen, the wily Guise, put on her proudest
    smile,
And busked her in her brawest gown, to march with
    the young Stock Geill.
    Sing hey Stock Geill! and ho Stock Geill! the
        old god and the new!
    We'll dash his bones against the stones, and
        shame the shaveling crew!

A marmoset! a marmoset! the Devil work them
    sorrow!

They've brought him from the Grey Friars, and
   nailed him to a barrow!
Then on their heads they lift him, and with sounding
   pomp they come,
With Latin rant, and snivelling chant, and pipe, and
   fife, and drum.
     Sing hey Stock Geill! and ho Stock Geill! this
      day the priests shall rue!
     Against the stones we'll dash the bones o' the
      idol painted new!

A marmoset! a marmoset! the puppet-god to show,
West about, and East about, and round about they go;
Along the Luckenbooths they trail, and down to big
   . Jack's Close,
And the bone of his arm, to work a charm, they kiss
   at the Abbey Cross!
     Sing hey Stock Geill! and ho Stock Geill! this
      kissing ye shall rue!
     We'll dash your bones against the stones, though
      you're painted fresh and new!

Now hold your god, ye shaveling loons!—for the
   queen she's gone to dine,

Full weary from the march, I ween, with Sandy
    Carpentine ;
There brews a storm betwixt the Bows—the crowd
    looks black and grim !
They rush !—they spring !—hold fast your god !
    they'll tear him limb from limb !
      Sing hey Stock Geill ! and ho Stock Geill ! this
        dainty godling new !
      They mass their bands, and with strong hands
        they'll do ! they'll do ! they'll do !

They rived the nails, they seized him by the feet,—I
    tell thee true—
They dashed his head against the stones—his stump
    in flinders flew !
Thou young Stock Geill, and wilt thou die, poor
    imp, and give no token ?
Thy father had a stouter skull, was not so lightly
    broken !
      Sing hey Stock Geill ! and ho Stock Geill ! the
        silly godling new !
      We dashed his bones against the stones, and his
        stump in flinders flew !

Then hurly burly! light as straw the priests were
    blown asunder;
They puffed and blew, they panted hot, they gaped
    with foolish wonder;
Down go their crosses! up their skirts! their caps fly
    in the air;
Their surplice flaps; they run as fast as them their
    legs can bear!
    Like crows at pop of gun, the grey and black-
    . stoled friars flew,
    Mid curse and sneer, and gibe and jeer, and
    merry wild halloo!

And so this gest was bravely done that gave the Pope
    a shog,
That now no stout Scotch knee might bend before a
    painted log!
The Devil's lumber-room we swept—for thus John
    Knox did say:
Pull down the rookery, and the rooks will quickly fly
    away!
    We left no trappings of Stock Geill; that day
    we ne'er shall rue,
    When we dashed his bones against the stones,
    and his stump in flinders flew!

THE SONG OF MRS JENNY GEDDES.[10]

Some praise the fair Queen Mary, and some the good
  Queen Bess,
And some the wise Aspasia, beloved by Pericles;
But o'er all the world's brave women, there's one that
  bears the rule,
The valiant Jenny Geddes, that flung the three-
  legged stool.
With a row-dow——at them now!—Jenny fling the
  stool!

'Twas the twenty-third of July, in the sixteen thirty-
  seven,
On Sabbath morn from high St Giles'. the solemn
  peal was given:

D

King Charles had sworn that Scottish men should
　　pray by printed rule;
He sent a book, but never dreamt of danger from a
　　stool.
With a row-dow—yes, I trow!—there's danger in a
　　stool!

The Council and the Judges, with ermined pomp
　　elate,
The Provost and the Bailies in gold and crimson state,
Fair silken-vested ladies, grave Doctors of the school,
Were there to please the King, and learn the virtue
　　of a stool.
With a row-dow—yes, I trow!—there's virtue in a stool!

The Bishop and the Dean came in wi' mickle gravity,
Right smooth and sleek, but lordly pride was lurking
　　in their e'e;
Their full lawn sleeves were blown and big, like seals
　　in briny pool;
They bore a book, but little thought they soon should
　　feel a stool.
With a row-dow—yes, I trow!—they'll feel a three
　　legged stool!

The Dean he to the altar went, and, with a solemn look,
He cast his eyes to heaven, and read the curious-
    printed book :
In Jenny's heart the blood upwelled with bitter
    anguish full ;
Sudden she started to her legs, and stoutly grasped
    the stool !
With a row-dow—at them now ! firmly grasp the stool !

As when a mountain wild-cat springs on a rabbit
    small,
So Jenny on the Dean springs, with gush of holy gall ;
Wilt thou say the mass at my lug, thou Popish-puling
    fool ?
No ! no ! she said, and at his head she flung the three-
    legged stool.
With a row-dow—at them now !—Jenny fling the stool !

A bump, a thump ! a smash, a crash ! now gentle
    folks beware !
Stool after stool, like rattling hail, came tirling through
    the air,
With, Well done, Jenny ! bravo, Jenny ! that's the
    proper tool !

When the Deil will out, and shows his snout, just
    meet him with a stool!
With a row-dow—at them now!—there's nothing like a
    stool!

The Council and the Judges were smitten with strange
    fear,
The ladies and the Bailies their seats did deftly clear,
The Bishop and the Dean went, in sorrow and in dool,
And all the Popish flummery fled, when Jenny
    showed the stool!
With a row-dow—at them now!—Jenny show the
    stool!

And thus a mighty deed was done by Jenny's valiant
    hand;
Black Prelacy and Popery she drave from Scottish
    land;
King Charles he was a shuffling knave, priest Laud a
    meddling fool,
But Jenny was a woman wise, who beat them with a
    stool!
With a row-dow—yes, I trow!—she conquered by the
    stool!

BOOK II.

POLYHYMNIA.

'Αναξιφόρμιγγες ὕμνοι
Τίνα θεὸν, τιν' ἥρωα, τίνα δ' ἄνδρα κελαδήσομεν.

—PINDAR.

Odi profanum vulgus et arceo.

—HORACE.

HYMN TO HELIOS.

Ἥλιον περιάγει ψυχή.—PLATO.

BEAUTIFUL orb, that rulest the sky, bright joy of
    creation,
Helios! oldest of gods, when earth, with divinity
    teeming,
Spake to the eye and the heart of a race that be-
    lieved in their feelings
Now they call thee a globe, a fiery sphere in the
    welkin,
Blindly wheeled, the causer of light, but wheeling
    in blindness;
Blindly wheeled by a law, with might despotic,
    compelling
Atoms, and suns, and moons, the dust that turneth
    the balance,

Clouds that float in the sky, and waves that swell in
　　the ocean.
Beautiful Sun ! whom millions worshipped, bright joy
　　of creation !
Still let me deem thee a god !—or, if potent Science
　　deny me
This heart-worship, which lived when men had faith
　　in their feelings,
I from Philosophy borrow a name to baptize thee—be
　　greeted,
Light-giving eye of the God, whose soul is the life of
　　the Cosmos !
Eye not seeing, like vision of men, with tamely re-
　　cipient
Organ, but causing to see, creative, procreant, plastic ;
Eye in which Plato believed, and the broad-viewed
　　thinkers of Hellas,
Ere mechanical men, with curious lines and triangles,
Measured the skies, and mapped the bald ungodded
　　creation ;
Eye of the welkin, I praise thee ! the glory that
　　waked in the Persian
Hymns of awful delight, and sent the Pelasgic
　　Apollo

Forth, a glorious youth, with golden locks down-flowing
Over the shoulders that bore the quiver with arrows
    resounding:
Me that glory inspires in the clime of the mist-
    wreathed mountain;
Me thy deity stirs in the land, where a jealous
    theology
Watches the words of the wise, and grudges free
    thought to the thinker.
I will praise thee; inspire my heart with flooding
    emotion!
Fill me with thoughts as rich as the leafy tree, which
    redundant
Shakes her tresses around, and waves her beauty
    before me!
Teach me to praise thee with skill, that whoso hears
    may adore thee,
Helios! beautiful orb, the plastic eye of creation!

　Beautiful Sun! when the procreant breath on the
    primal waters
Brooded, divinely stirring the crude and weltering
    Chaos,
Water, and earth, and air, and fire, in dim elemental

Strife inorganic convolved, and rolling in huge con-
  fusion,
Then thou wert not, beautiful Sun! but evident
  darkness
Struggled with fitfullest fire, in dismal yawning abysses
Joyless. Forth from the thought of the all-creative
  Jehovah
Walked thy luminous round with intelligential clear-
  ness.
Chaos before thee fled; the vast convolutions of
  darkness
Rolled away; the elements, freed from tangled em-
  broilment,
Grouped their atoms, and sought in kindred classes to
  mingle.
Thou, bright eye of the world, didst order the infinite
  discord,
Thou, first servant of God, the Supreme Causer of
  order!
Moulded by thee in the slimy swathes of mud primeval,
Struggled the formative life in the plant; thy ray
  calorific
Fashioned the germs of growth, and shapes of exuberant beauty

Sprang from the bursting clod with leafy splendour
    enfolden.
Gently the blade of the grass came creeping over the
    meadow;
Stately rose the tree; and in graceful rings sym-
    metric,
Spread the fresh-green fern its fan to the zephyr
    gigantic.
Beautiful world! from year to year in gladness I
    greet thee;
Yearly the power of the Spring, and the ray of the
    life-dispensing
Glorious Sun invests the old and hoary creation
Fresh in juvenile green; and yearly my heart within
    me
Beats to the pulses that stirred, when Helios moulded
    the Cosmos.
Beautiful trees! that with far-sent fangs securely
    rooted,
Clasp the rock, and with rounded stems, erect and
    stable,
Rise to the light; then swinging your arms with
    opulent leafage
Broadly tufted, or finely needled, drooping or spreading,

Sway to the breeze : ye forests, that wave with various
    grandeur,
Dark with the veteran pine, or light with the taper-
    ing larch-tree,
Stout with the bunchy plane, or soft with the fine-
    leaved linden,
Smooth with beech, or rough with the large-flowered
    spears of the chestnut,
Fragrant with pendulous birch, the white-stemmed
    pride of the dark brown
Mountain torrent, that scoops the shelvy bed of the mica :
Praised be the beauty of trees ! them Helios brought
    from the darkness,
Cherished their seeds -in the rift of the rock, and
    lustily reared them,
Richly with verdure to clothe the old grey sides of the
    mountain.
Beautiful flowers ! the joy of the meadow, the grace
    of the garden,
Triumph of genial light, disparted in colour, and scattered
Wide o'er the verdure of earth, with beneficent wild
    profusion,
Wonderful ! filling the eye with continuous feasts,
    and the heart with

Thrills of dainty delight ! Full oft in your quest I have
    wandered
Deep into murkiest woods, and high where the pin-
    nacled granite
Shelters the snow through the summer, and far where
    the cataract thunders
Over the storm-seamed brow of the grim-indented
    mountain :
There the bell, and the cup, and the purple star have
    found me,
Beautiful, crowning with life the forehead of bleak
    desolation,
Smiling, like children's eyes, with miraculous light
    from the deep black
Yawning chasm, that seemed an abode for barrenness
    only.
Beautiful flowers ! or gemming the snow-wreathed
    hills, or at random
Spotting with vegetive gold the broad fat fields of
    the lowland,
Nodding in airy clusters aloft, or broad as a buckler,
Floating in lazy pride on the bosom of deep slow waters,
'Neath hot tropical suns ; in lowliest guise, like the
    sorrel

Shading its delicate tints 'neath the moss-grown stumps
    of the forest,
Or in magnificent globes high-blown, with petal on
    petal,
Closely-massed, and cunningly cut into curious splen-
    dour,
Looking in face of the Sun with the vermeil pomp of
    the Summer;
Lovely parade of beautiful growth, divinely unfolden
World of colour, I bless thee, and praise the Creator
    who gave me
Eyes to drink in the light, and share thy magical
    fountain,
Helios, beautiful orb, the plastic eye of creation !

    Beautiful Earth ! in vesture of various light en-
    veloped,
Glorious ! ever to me thy beauty has been as a garden
Gemmed with flowery delight, and breathing odorous
    sweetness !
Ever new wonder hath thrilled my wondering eye,
    beholding
Each soft line of thy grace, each ample front of thy
    grandeur.

Oft with vagabond foot thy fields I have traversed at
    random,
Free, with savage delight, by modes and fashions un-
    cumbered,
Nourishing thoughts as light as the gull that floats
    o'er the billow,
Breezy and fresh as the Zephyr that tosses the green
    and plumy
Glory of trees in the light, and pouring unsought and
    unhindered
Hymns of vital delight! I praise thee, God, and
    thy sunlit
Earth, the garden of man, as abroad I wander in
    fancy,
Viewing again and again thy wealth of wonderful
    pictures,
Hung in the halls of the soul by thy magical many-
    hued mirror,
Memory, mother of Thought! And now my fantasy
    lifts me
Far to the lands of the South, where Light, like a
    queen majestic,
Sways with sovereign strength, and smiles with broad,
    diffusive,

Liberal brightness unsullied; and there the bluff
  rock-forehead
Stands in the flash of the sea, high-crowned with
  the nicely-measured
Marble pillars, as white as the flower which bursts in
  the morning,
Hung with memories of worship as fair as the light
  which surrounds them,
Dian, or radiant Apollo, or she, the blue-eyed
  virgin,
Daughter of Jove, strong-fathered, with weighty
  spear and buckler
Bright, far-glancing, a sign to the worn sea-wandering
  sailor.
There my fantasy lifts me, and there on sun-woven
  pictures
Feeds and fattens with joy. Or me, with a turn of
  my musing,
Suddenly thought transports to the castled crags of
  the Rhine stream,
Terraced with vines, and brewing by mystic brewst of
  the sun-light
Wine, which gladdens the heart: and there I see in
  the arbour

Knots of men and women, the gentle, the kind, and
    the thoughtful,
Feasting on sunny delights, and the sportive freak of
    the moment,
Harmless-bubbling; or wandering far through mazes
    of leafy
Copse-wood wild, and making the old grey ruin re-
    echo
Free with songs, the voice of an easy sweet-blooded
    people,
Plain, unbribed by the cumbersome pride which fetters
    the Briton.
These thy pictures, O Sun! the living, the varied,
    the changing
Ever, but ever the same, wide-spread in magnificent
    fulness
Wonderful! Who can declare the wealth of lumi-
    nous glory,
Flowing in radiant oceans, where stars are wheeling
    in mazes
Vast, uncounted, unscanned by the glass of the far-
    sighted gazer?
Me such glory confounds. I rather, with wise limi-
    tation,

Feed on the shows of truth, and chiefly the sights of
    my dear-loved
Strong Caledonian home, the land of the flood and
    the mountain.
Beautiful Scotland! or where thy broad hills, smooth,
    green-mantled,
Sink to the vale, far fringed with the pomp of man-
    sion and villa,
Rich, well-gardened; or where the might of thy
    Grampian rises
High, far-sweeping, majestic, and flushing far with
    the purple
Springy heather, deer-trodden. How blest to the foot
    is the labour,
High from thy breezy heath to brush the dew, Cale-
    donia!
Whether pursuing the stag to his haunt on the lone,
    rock-girdled
Mountain tarn, or regaling the eye with grandeur of
    high-piled
Peak on peak, and feasting the ear with music of
    waters
Rushing adown birch-glens, where the trout in the
    amber caldron

Shoots as swift as a fresh young thought from the
    brain of the thinker.

Here thy glories, O Sun, in the shifting play of the
    shadow,

Thousandfold varied, appear, when the skirt of the
    delicate-floating

Mist now rests on a crag, now round a black tremendous

Precipice skirs, as swift as the rush of dreams in a
    dreamer.

Oft on a broad bare mount, Bencleugh, or lofty
    Muicdhui,

Sombre hangs a pall of dark dense cloud from the
    welkin;

Sombre the traveller looks, the unwearied climber of
    mountains,

All his prospect is dimmed, the glory of hills is de-
    parted.

Sudden the curtain uprises; beneath the rim of the
    dark cloud

Luminous shines the carpeted plain; the silvery land-
    scape

Glorious glistens along the line of the shimmering river;

Castle and crag gleam out; the old grey-centuried
    turret

Rises over the wood; the white-washed cottage is
    glinting
Far through the dark-blue pine; the spire in the
    village is twinkling
Bright in the Sun; the vents of the populous far-
    spreading city
Shoot their white-blue fumes in beautiful scrolls to
    the welkin,
Telling of labour and power, and thought, the mighty
    magician.
Such thy glories, O Light, on the broad brown moun-
    tains of Scotland!
Such thy wonderful sleight on the pictured face of
    the high-land,
Helios, beautiful orb, the plastic eye of creation!

    Beautiful Light! the child from the rayless womb
        of its mother
Sudden emerging, and claiming his lot in a larger
    existence,
Free, self-rooted, self-centred, from thee, thou centre
    of gladness,
Knows the beneficent thrill that quickens the sensuous
    nervlets,

Delicate, timorous, soon to embrace with miraculous
  grasping
Realms of measureless knowledge.   By thee the full-
  grown thinker
Nurses his ken, and learns to be wise by looking and
  loving,
Clearly scanning the smallest, and widely surveying
  the largest
Forms of exuberant life, with a full and ripe compre-
  hension.
Thine is the circle of Being; the bond art thou
  that unitest
Nearest and farthest of things with a potent function,
  electric,
Wonder-working. By Thee the Earth with the
  Heaven communeth,
Knowing with known, and lover with loved; and
  through infinite spaces
Star sends message to star, and comet shoots greeting
  to comet.
Beautiful Light! with cunning disposal of lens and
  of mirror
Science may torture thy forms, and question thy
  Protean splendour,

Call thee a radiant matter, or feel thy quivering
    pulses,
Telling of rise and of fall in the undulant flow of thy
    beauty.
Me this beauty suffices. I look, and enjoy, and adore
    thee,
Godlike, born of a God, with virtue divinest re-
    dundant !
Father of lights, receive this lisping hymn of my
    worship ;
Thou first Sun of all suns, first glory of glories, and
    only
Substance of all that seems, prime mover of all that
    moveth,
Fill my heart with thy brightness, and teach me with
    open receptive
Faculty ever to live on the fulness of beauty around
    me !
Teach me ever to thrill to the breath of thy grace, as
    a well-tuned
Harp responds to the touch of a subtle and dexterous
    harper.
Thus no discord shall master my fate ; and in har-
    mony sweetest

Human shall chime with divine.   Thus teach me, O
    Father, to praise thee !
Thee, the source of all life, and thy Sun, the joy of
    all living,
High hung up for a sign in the hall of the glorious
    Cosmos,
Helios ! beautiful orb, the plastic eye of creation !

JOHN THE BAPTIST.

Who is he in hairy raiment
    Clad, i' the wilderness
Preaching freely without payment
    Truth and righteousness ?
Whoso hears, and not despises,
Him with water he baptizes,
    In the contrite hour ;
Whoso hears with haughty scorning,
Him he smites with holy warning,
    And with prophet's power.

Swarms the city from its corners,
    Motley bad and good ;
Thoughtless hearts and hoary mourners
    Haste to Jordan's flood :
Some for sin their souls abasing ;
Some to feed their eye with gazing ;
    Some to search and try

With captious craft the shaggy preacher,
And themselves to teach the teacher ;
   Some they know not why.

Comes the Rabbi, with a stately,
   Measured gravity ;
With a solemn air, sedately
   Comes the Pharisee ;
Wide his robe, and on the border
Sacred texts, in well-marched order,
   Show his purpose plain,
With a nice and fenced existence,
Far to keep, at holy distance,
   Every touch profane.

Came fat priest, and pontiff portly,
   With a bloated face ;
Came Herodian, smooth and courtly,
   With a gay grimace.
Came the Essene from his station
Of secluded contemplation
   With mild gravity ;
With an eye of twinkling keenness,
And a smile of cold sereneness,
   Came the Sadducee.

Came the soldier firm and steady,
    Frolicsome and gay,
With his quick hand ever ready
    For the rising fray.
Came the usurer, dry and meagre,
Came the publican, sharp and eager
    For great Cæsar's penny.
With a train of silken pages
Comes the rich man; with scant wages
    Come the burdened many.

What saith he, the wayside preacher,
    To this motley crew?
Doth he come a cunning teacher
    Of lore strange and new?
Hath he drawn without omission,
Point for point, a long confession,
    To inform the brain?
Piled a proud word-architecture,
Fenced it round with nice conjecture,
    And distinctions vain?

Hath he wove a girth to measure
    God, a chain to bind

The Infinite, and mapped at leisure
    The omniscient Mind?
Hath he trimmed an old theogony,
Cumbrous rear'd a new cosmogony,
    To employ the schools?
Not with speculation vainest
Preacheth he;—with wisdom plainest,
    And with simplest rules.

Thus he speaks—" Repent ! Repentance
    Smooths Messiah's way;
'Tis an old and weighty sentence,
    Weigh it well to-day.
Hast thou nursed a sin ?—confess it ;
Hast thou done a wrong ?—redress it :
    And, with just desire,
Ask no more than what is due thee :
Be content, when offer'd to thee,
    With thy lawful hire.

" Say not, with vain pride elated,
    ' God's own people we,
Tracing high a hoary-dated
    Patriarch pedigree.'

Peopled earth is thickly studded
With the children common-blooded,
    Of the great I AM.
From the hard flint, at his pleasure,
God can raise up without measure
    Sons to Abraham.

" Hear, whose barren trunk hath cumber'd
    Now too long the ground,
Saith the Lord, your days are number'd ;
    Hark ! with crashing sound,
Falls the axe that fells the fruitless !
Toils he not with labour bootless
    Who now smites the tree.
He his winnow'd wheat shall garner,
But like empty chaff the scorner
    Burn with fire shall he."

Thus he preached to great and small men,
    Of the human right;
Like the blessed sun, on all men
    Shedding simple light.
O ! wise are they who hear such preaching,
Not too high for common teaching
    In life's common ways ;

Not with proud pretence ballooning,
Not with gay parade festooning,
    To catch the vulgar gaze.

Flap who will the air-borne pinion,
    Sweeping far and free;
Solid earth be my dominion,
    Baptist John, with thee!
In the plainest path of duty,
Stamping daily things with beauty,
    I with thee will tread;
Where thy warning finger pointed
I would follow, where the anointed
    Saviour lowly led!

BEAUTIFUL WORLD.

Beautiful world!
  Though bigots condemn thee,
My tongue finds no words
  For the graces that gem thee!
Beaming with sunny light,
  Bountiful ever,
Streaming with gay delight,
  Full as a river!
        Bright world! brave world!
          Let cavillers blame thee!
        I bless thee, and bend
          To the God who did frame thee!

Beautiful world !
  Bursting around me,
Manifold, million-hued
  Wonders confound me !
From earth, sea, and starry sky,
  Meadow and mountain,
Eagerly gushes
  Life's magical fountain.
      Bright world ! brave world !
        Though witlings may blame thee,
        Wonderful excellence
        Only could frame thee !

The bird in the greenwood
  His sweet hymn is trolling,
The fish in blue ocean
  Is spouting and rolling !
Light things on airy wing,
  Wild dances weaving,
Clods with new life in spring
  Swelling and heaving !
      Thou quick-teeming world,
        Though scoffers may blame thee,
        I wonder, and worship
        The God who could frame thee !

Beautiful world!
  What poesy measures
Thy strong-flooding passions,
  Thy light-trooping pleasures?
Mustering, marshalling,
  Striving and straining,
Conquering, triumphing,
  Ruling and reigning!
      Thou bright-armied world!
        So strong!—who can tame thee?
      Wonderful power of God
        Only could frame thee!

Beautiful world!
  While godlike I deem thee,
No cold wit shall move me
  With bile to blaspheme thee!
I have lived in thy light,
  And, when Fate ends my story,
May I leave on death's cloud
  The bright trail of life's glory!
      Wondrous old world!
        No ages shall shame thee!
      Ever bright with new light
        From the God who did frame thee!

THE WOOD-SORREL.[11]

FAIR flower, beneath the dark fir-tree
Shaded in delicate pudency,
I'll make a little rhyme to thee,
    (Some years I owe it):
Pansies and lilies have their praises,
Small celandines and broad-faced daisies;
But thou, sweet sorrel of the woods,
The tenderest grace of solitudes,
    I do not know it,
If thou hast stirred the deeper moods
    Of any poet.

Thou'rt like a maiden in the bud,
Bashful, ere life's full-swelling flood
Hath shot into the outer blood
    A bolder feeling.

F

Thy trefoil shield thou spread'st before thee,
That I to find thy flower bend o'er thee,
And wonder how so lowly there
Was set a gem so pure, so fair,
    Such charms concealing :
For why should God create the fair
    But for revealing ?

Yet have I seen both fair and good
I' the perfect bloom of womanhood,
Who, like thyself, the light eschewed,
    Thou wood-nymph fairest !
And wept to think how foplings shallow
Left such deep quiet virtue fallow,
To feed vain gaze on flaunting show
Of painted things, in formal row,
    The coldest, barest ;
While thou, low-veiled, and nodding low,
    Wert blushing rarest.

And God, who planted thee, was wise,
I' the shade—no vulgar-vended prize
For men, whose love is in their eyes,
    And goes no deeper :

Better for thee, and such as thou art,
To be the forest-nun thou now art,
Than yoked to some loose-dangling mate
Whom thou canst neither love nor hate,
    Thy body's keeper,
But to thy sweet soul's estimate
    Blind, or a sleeper.

Me may the God who sways the heart
Wean more from each false flaring art,
And still some modest truth impart
    Through thy revealing!
As, yearly, sooty crowds eschewing,
The fragrant fresh May-breezes wooing,
My footed pilgrimage I make
Through wood and wold, and passive take
    Each vagrant feeling,
Which thou, and such as thou, can wake
    With balmy healing.

SABBATH EVENING IN ETTRICK.

How softly on the broad green hill
　　The golden Eve is sleeping,
While, through the vale below, how still
　　The cool grey shade is creeping!
The cuckoo's vesper from the wood
　　Floats sweetly through the shadow;
The stream, as mild as maidenhood,
　　Is wimpling through the meadow,
　　　　This Sabbath eve!

O Thou, who workest peace from strife
　　By organizing spirit,
Whose eye hath fathomed all the life
　　Which mortal men inherit,

Soothe thou my thought, and in my mind
    Rule each distempered motion,
That I may love thy law, and find
    Sweet peace with meek devotion,
        Each Sabbath eve !

THE COTTAGE MANSE.[12]

The little cot on the hill side
        So brown and bare,
The lonely cot all white and trim,
On the swift mountain torrent's brim,
Where the old ash-tree's shattered pride
Tells tales of many a storm defied—
        Who liveth there?

Who liveth there?—no common man,
        A man of God.
Though now within this lowly cot
He shares the humble peasant's lot,
Late, when a public-stationed man,
A large house on a goodly plan ,
        Was his abode.

A minister of sacred things,
    He bound together,
By higher ties than human law,
The men that shared his faith with awe ;
He had his seat at power's right hand,
And lords and ladies of the land
    Did call him brother.

But when a fatal strife arose,
    Hard choice compelling,
Snapping old bonds of Church and State,
Not with himself held he debate,
But with a faithful foot unbought,
He with his loved ones sadly sought
    This low-roofed dwelling.

And here he lives, and serves his God
    On this bare spot ;
And, though no more in pride he stand
Before the mighty of the land,
A dear and a devoted few
Surround with love, and service true,
    His humble cot.

ELLISLAND.[13]

FAIR Ellisland, thou dearest spot
On Scottish soil to each true Scot,
With wood and stream, and shining cot,
    Thy beauty sways me,
And love is rash—O blame me not,
    If I shall praise thee !

Wide waves the leafy June around,
The banks with blossomy curls are crowned,
Sweet flows with mild and murmurous sound
    The clear Nith river,
And Peace holds all the grassy ground
    Now sacred ever.

ELLISLAND.

The poet's farm !—a fairer sight
Ne'er filled my view with calm delight ;
Full fitly here our minstrel wight
    Did pitch his dwelling,
With Beauty's green and gentle might
    Around him swelling !

Here stands the house, the very wall
Stout labour raised at Robin's call,
A farmer's beild, which, low and small,
    No envy breedeth,
Enough for comfort, and for all
    A poet needeth.

And there the stack-yard, where he lay
And gazed upon the starry ray,
When pensive Memory's tender sway,
    With fingers fairy,
Struck from his heart the sad sweet lay
    Of Highland Mary !

And here the bank where he did sit,
When once his quick and glancing wit
Off-started on a racing fit
    With glorious canter,

And forth with flashing hit on hit
    Flew Tam O'Shanter !

And oft, I ween, to that green bower
He walked, in placid evening hour,
With bonnie Jean, whose smile had power
    To soothe his spirit,
When fitful thoughts, and fancies sour,
    Might rudely stir it !

Fair Ellisland, thou dearest spot
To each true-hearted stalwarth Scot,
When I forget thy small white cot
    And winding river,
Sheer from my thought may Memory blot
    All trace for ever !

THE JUNGFRAU OF THE LURLEI.[14]

(A LEGEND OF THE RHINE.)

Who sails with pennant waving gay
   So swift adown the Rhine ?—
A chief I see with ostrich plume,
   A chief and boatmen nine.

As swallow swift with dipping wing,
   So swift they glide along,
And ever as they lift the oar
   They raise the merry song.

It is the young Count Palatine
   That fares in that swift boat,
And he a deed of strange intent
   Within his heart hath thought.

For he hath heard of the Jungfrau
That on the Lurlei stands,
And he in haste is coming now
On her to lay his hands.

By Mary Mother hath he sworn,
The maiden shall be mine—
Now fresh to work, my merry men,
And row we down the Rhine!

The pilot was an aged man :
Deep thought with blithe content
Upon his weather-beaten brow
And cheek was friendly blent.

"I rede thee, young Count Palatine,
I rede thee well," quoth he,
"I am a man of many years,
Though but of low degree.

"I rede thee well, Count Palatine,
My spirit bodes no good
Of this strange voyage that we sail ;
We do not as we should.

" The virgin of the Lurlei rock,
   We know not what she be :
She may be of the angel race;
   She is no bride for thee.

" Or an Undine she may be,
   A daughter of the stream ;
Rough mortal hand to touch a maid
   So pure may not beseem.

" For ofttimes at calm eventide,
   As native fishers tell,
When mellow shines the parting light,
   And chimes the vesper bell,

" She beckons with a friendly hand,
   And, pointing to the flood,
There, if you fish, she seems to say,
   Your fishing will be good.

" And whoso, with the rising sun,
   First casts where she hath shown,
The choicest fish that Rhine can boast
   That day he calls his own.

"I rede thee well, Count Palatine,
   My heart misgives me sore,
I rede thee, turn from this Jungfrau,
   And think on her no more."

"Have thou no fear, my pilot true,
   Thou know'st I mean no harm,
The maid shall grace my festal board,
   Shall rest within my arm.

"And be she of Undine tribe,
   Or of the angel race,
The Heaven that gave the heart to dare,
   Shall crown the deed with grace!"

And to his words a loud halloo
   His merry comrades shouted;
The pilot strove to smile in vain;
   He shook his head, and doubted.

And plash, and plash, and hil-hilloa!
   Still gaily on it goes
Adown the stream, till to their view
   The Lurlei rock uprose.

And on that rock there shone a sheen
   Of mingled sun and moon,
And as they nigher came, they heard
   A strange unearthly tune,

But wondrous sweet. The Jungfrau sate
   Beside the silver sand,
And held a string of amber-beads
   In her uplifted hand.

And her the mellow-setting sun
   And mellow-rising moon
Beshone, as moveless there she sate,
   And sang her witching tune.

"Now, by high Heaven! that golden hair,
   That eye of blue is mine!"—
So spake, and sprang with sudden leap
   The young Count Palatine;

But sprang too soon. His hasty step
   Missed the deceiving shore:
The whirling eddy sucked him down;
   He sank, and rose no more.

" Saint Ursel, save us !" cried the men,
   And rowed them up the Rhine :
The maid was seen no more that night,
   Nor more the moon did shine.

The Count was wroth ; he loved his son :
   Three trusty knights sent he,
To seize that Jungfrau, and revenge
   Her wicked sorcerie.

For he did deem the childe was drowned
   By cursed craft of hell ;
Three holy red-cross knights he sent,
   To break that fiendish spell.

The three knights came. The Jungfrau read
   Their message on their face ;
" Touch me no mortal hand, for I
   Am of Undine race !"

She said, and in the deep blue wave
   Her amber-beads she threw—
" Come, father !—welcome, watery home ;
   Ungrateful earth, adieu !"

The waves did swell, the waves did roll,
   The waves did heave them high;
Into twin foamy steeds their crests
   Did shape them fearfully.

And on the one a king there sate,
   Old Kühleborn he hight;
He wore an emerald mantle green,
   With pearls his crown was dight.

A sceptre of the watery reed
   His outstretched arm did wave,
And with an eye of ocean's blue,
   A strong command he gave.

And she, the daughter of his love,
   Besprang the second steed,
And louted low before her sire,
   Who helped her in her need.

The waves fell back, the waves fell down;
   Into their caves they coil;
As if by Jesu's voice rebuked,
   Their face lay calm as oil.

The knights beheld it from the rock,
   Their knees sink down in prayer,
And signing many a holy cross,
   Unto their boats they fare.

And on the cradled wave upborne
   A silver shell they saw;
A shining text was writ thereon,
   They read that text with awe.

" Think twice, rash man, before thy foot
   Disturb a holy spot;
The lovely shapes of earth and sky
   Behold—but touch them not !"

THE COVENANTER'S LAMENT.

O WALY waly up the glen,
  And waly waly o'er the moor!
The land is full of bloody men,
  Who hunt to death the friendless poor!
We brook the rule of robbers wild;
  They tear the son from his father's lands,
They tear the mother from her child,
  They tear the Bible from our hands!

Last night, as I came o'er the moor,
  And stood upon the grey hill-crown,
I saw the red flames rise wi' power
  Frae the lone house o' Alik Brown.
The godless grim dragoons were there,
  And Clavers spake, that swearing loon,
" So burn the nest, so smoke the lair
  Of all that dare to think wi' Brown !"

O blessed Lord, who rul'st in Heaven,
   Who preached thy gospel to the poor,
How long shall thy best friends be driven
   Like hunted hares from moor to moor?
Arise, O Lord, thy saints deliver,
   This land from ruthless despots free!
'Neath wintry skies we sit and shiver,
   But times of gladness come from thee!

SONG OF THE WINDS.

Blow! blow! blow!
By the eagle's rocky dwelling,
From Fairfield to Helvellyn,
    Blow! blow!
O'er the tempest's leafless track,
From Helvellyn to Saddleback.
    Blow! blow!

Blow! blow! blow!
Where the thunder loud is pealing,
Round the shepherd's lonely shieling,
    Blow! blow!
Where the torrent wildly dashing,
With white flail the rock is lashing,
    Blow! blow!

Blow! blow! blow!
O'er the grey and rocky ruin,
Where black cloud is cloud pursuing,
Blow! blow!
Like demons, with sharp yell,
When they hunt a soul to hell,
Blow! blow!

Blow! blow! blow!
Where the traveller on the hill
Wanders blindly without skill,
Blow! blow!
Whom suddenly a blast
Down the sheer black wall shall cast,
Blow! blow!

Blow! blow! blow!
Where the sapless leaves are whirling,
Where the ruddy floods are swirling,
Blow! blow!
Where the farmer's yellow store
Floats to sea with rush and roar,
Blow! blow!

Blow ! blow ! blow !
Where the drowning man is calling
Through the storm's relentless brawling,
Blow ! blow !
Where with planks and drifted dead
Wide the wreathèd sands are spread,
Blow ! blow !

Blow ! blow ! blow !
With mist, and rain, and rack,
From Scawfell to Saddleback,
Blow ! blow !
Who shall check you in the hour,
When God arms your wings with power ?
Blow ! blow !

MOMENTS.

In the beauty of life's budding,
  When young pulses beat with hope,
And a purple light is flooding
  Round thought's blossoms as they ope;
When the poet's song is dearest,
  And, where sacred anthems swell,
Every word of power thou hearest
  Holds thy spirit like a spell;
        O these are moments, fateful moments,
        Big with issue—use them well!

When a sudden gust hath tumbled
  Hope's bright architecture down;
When some prouder fair hath humbled
  Thy proud passion with a frown;
When thy dearest friends deceive thee,
  And cold looks thy love repel,

And the bitter humours grieve thee,
  That make God's fair earth a hell;
    O these are moments, trying moments,
    Meant to try thee—use them well!

When a flash of truth hath found thee,
  Where thy foot in darkness trod,
When thick clouds dispart around thee,
  And thou standest nigh to God.
When a noble soul comes near thee,
  In whom kindred virtues dwell,
That from faithless doubts can clear thee,
  And with strengthening love compel;
    O these are moments, rare fair moments;
    Sing and shout, and use them well!

When a haughty threat hath cowed thee,
  And with weak, unmanly shame,
Ignoble thou hast bowed thee
  To the terror of a name;
And then God holds the mirror
  Where thy better self doth dwell,
And thou dost start with terror,
  And thy tears gush like a well;

O these are moments, blessèd moments ;
Weep and pray, and use them well !

In the pride of thy succeeding,
  When, beneath thy high command,
Every soul must own the leading
  Of thy strong-controlling hand ;
When wide cheers of acclamation
  Round thy march of triumph swell,
And the plaudits of a nation
  Every thought of fear expel ;
    O these are moments, slippery moments ;
    Watch and pray, and use them well !

When the term of life hath found thee,
  And thou smilest upon Fate,
And the golden sheaves around thee
  For the angels' sickle wait ;
When the pure love thou achievest
  Doth the mortal pang expel,
And a shining track thou leavest
  To dear friends that love thee well ;
    O these are moments, happy moments ;
    Bless God, with whom all issues dwell !

THE SCOTSMAN'S VOCATION.

Thou sturdy Scottish man,
Still be first in labour's van!
'Tis the mission of the Highest, given visibly to Thee!
With the hammer and the spade
Ply thine earth-subduing trade,
And thou shalt be a prince at home, and a king
beyond the sea!

Where the ragged thistle grows,
There dig, and plant the rose,
And make a blooming garden on the bare hill side!
Beneath the leafy shade
Which thine own hands have made,
There claim thy sweatful honours, there nurse thy
sturdy pride!

By Thee the Titan steam
Hove the wonder-working beam,
Whose sway is like a thousand horses prancing in
their pride !
The smoking ships from Thee
Went forth that flap the sea,
Where the halls of merchant princes fringe the banks
of busy Clyde.

Thou sturdy Scottish man,
Since the Earth to wheel began,
There was heavy work to do by land, and heavy work
by sea ;
Still be faithful to thy plan,
And the GOD, who works by man,
Hath many a task of world-transforming toil in store
for Thee !

TRUST IN GOD.

Oft on the various-chequered Earth,
When dulled with care or flushed with mirth,
This feeble thought will force its birth,
    Tainting the heart with weariness—
Why should weak mortals toil and sweat
For goods, that vex the few who get,
Why for light baubles vainly fret,
    That gleam through wastes of dreariness?
Then the old Tempter, standing nigh,
Mutters, our staggering faith to try,
Go, Sinner, curse thy God and die,
    And leave this world of weariness!

Father supreme, whose sleepless might
Guides the vast planets in their flight,
Who dost alternate stated night
    With light, and joy, and cheerfulness ;
Who mak'st thy verdurous grass to grow
On hills, where sky-fed fountains flow,
Still bringing Summer's glorious show
    From bleak-browed Winter's fearfulness !
Thou, when such peevish thoughts intrude,
Teach me to wait in mute mild mood,
Till in my soul thee seemeth good
    To ope new founts of cheerfulness !

THE SABBATH-DAY.

The Sabbath-day, the Sabbath-day,
How softly shines the morn!
How gently from the heathery brae
The fresh hill-breeze is borne!
Sweetly the village bell doth toll,
And thus it seems to say,
Come rest thee, rest thee, weary soul,
On God's dear Sabbath-day!

Swift as the shifting pictures flit
Unscanned, unnoticed by,
To those who in the steam-car sit
And pass with rapid eye;
So flits our life with sweeping haste,
And hath no power to stay;

But GOD makes man his favoured guest
  On each dear Sabbath-day:

And to high converse doth invite
  The soul with tranquil eye
That numbers well, and marks aright
  The moments as they fly;
The soul that will not lawless roam,
  Nor with blind hurry stray,
But with itself would be at home
  On a peaceful Sabbath-day.   ·

There are who live as in a fair,
  The light, the shallow-hearted,
Nor ask or whither bound, or where
  They stand, or whence they started.
Aimless they live, and thoughtless fling
  Their rattling lives away,
Nor know to poise the brooding wing
  On a sober Sabbath-day.

Such judge I not. But me not so
  GOD made for light-wing'd prattle:
A soldier I, and I must know
  Before I fight, my battle.

I with the jingling bells an hour
  Would sport, then steal away,
To feel with truth, and plan with power
  On a thoughtful Sabbath-day.

Stern Scottish people, ye redeem
  Each seventh day severely;
Sober and grave, with scarce a gleam
  Of frolic tempered cheerly.
Light wits deride your thoughtful law,
  The tinkling and the gay;
But wisely from deep founts ye draw
  Calm strength on the Sabbath-day.

And safely, if I err, I err,
  Who on this day with you
The hot-spurred bustle and the stir
  Of dinsome life eschew.
Happy, if through the frequent dark
  Of man's tumultuous way,
God in my soul shall light a spark
  On his dear Sabbath-day.

SABBATH MORNING HYMN.

(Written at Farnham, Surrey.)

~~~~~~~~~~

FRESH blows the Autumn breeze ; wide waves
  The tawny-mantled corn ;
And wandering o'er far-stretching woods,
    The minstrel bell,
    With hollow swell,
Proclaims the Sabbath morn.

Hard-working England, hear the sound,
  And give thy panting heart
Its weekly rest, well-earned by toil :
    Harsh cares dismiss,
    And learn what bliss
God's Sabbath may impart
~~~~~~~~~~

To well-tuned souls.—Come cheerly forth
  From labour's grimy dens,
Ye sternly striving, and behold
    The bright sun shine,
    With power divine,
  On the green glades and glens

Of this fair Saxon land. Have time
  To breathe, and to employ
The soul on its own wealth; unbind
    Your work-day mail,
    And blithely hail
  One day of thoughtful joy.

Lo! where the white-smocked peasants flock
  To swell the morning prayer!
'Tis sweet to nurse high thoughts alone,
    But kindly wise,
    Not thou despise,
  The general hymn to share

Of kindred human hearts. What though
  Their creed, mayhap, from thine
Be far, one God, one heart, belongs

To all the clan,
Whose name is man,
One common blood divine.

Go thou, and join the song of love
And brotherhood, and pray
That pride and every prideful work
Be far from us ;
And hallow thus
Our English Sabbath-day.

ADVICE TO A FAVOURITE STUDENT ON LEAVING COLLEGE.

Dear youth, grey books no blossoms bear ;
  Thou hast enough of learning ;
For life's green fields thy march prepare,
  And take my friendly warning.
I would not have thee longer stay,
  To read of others' striving ;
Wield thine own arm !—the only way
  To know life is by living.

The brain's a small part of a man ;
  Though thought has wide dominions,
Thou canst not lift the smallest stone
  By Speculation's pinions.

Who learns an art by lifeless rule,
    Through mists will still be blinking;
The subtlest thinker is a fool,
    Who spins mere webs of thinking.

The times are feverish; mark me well!
    Have faith and patience by thee;
Unless thou curl into thy shell,
    Thou'lt find enough to try thee.
But that's a weak device.   I know
    Thou'lt face it free and fearless;
But O! beware the greater foe,
    A spirit proud and prayerless!

I love a bold and venturous boy,
    Who, full of fresh emotion,
Launches with large and liberal joy
    On life's wide-rolling ocean.
But there are rocks; and blind to steer
    Were thoughtless folly's merit:
Curb thou thy force with holy fear,
    And keep a watchful spirit.

Where eager crowds contend for pelf,
    The seller and the buyer,

Each one free range seeks for himself,
   And cares for nothing higher.
Make honey in an ordered hive,
   Nor join the lawless scramble
Of men, with whom in life to thrive
   Is with good luck to gamble.

We live in days when all would climb
   With hot, high-strung employment;
Some rage in prose, some writhe in rhyme,
   All hate a calm enjoyment.
Freedom's the watchword of the hour;
   But O! 'tis melancholy
When every bubbling brain has power
   To drown calm thought with folly!

The age is full of talkers.   Thou
   Be silent for a season,
Till slowly-ripening facts shall grow
   Into a stable reason.
Pert witlings fling crude fancies round,
   As wanton whim conceits them,
Pleased when from fools the echoed sound
   Of their own folly greets them.

Nurse thou, where eager babble spreads,
  A quiet brooding nature,
Nor strive, by lopping taller heads,
  To raise thy lesser stature.
Eschew the cavilling critic's art,
  The lust of loud reproving;
The brain by knowledge grows, the heart
  Is larger made by loving.

All things we cannot know. At sea
  As when a good ship saileth,
Our steps within the planks are free,
  Beyond, all cunning faileth.
So man as by a living bond
  Of circling powers is bounded;
Within the line is ours, beyond
  The sharpest wit's confounded.

What thing thou knowest, nicely know
  With curious fine dissection;
The smallest mite can something show
  That chains thy rapt inspection.
Allwhere with holy caution move,
  In God thy life is moving;

All things with reverent patience prove,
    'Tis God's will thou art proving.

What thing thou doest, bravely do;
    When Heaven's clear call hath found thee,
Follow!—with fervid wheels pursue,
    Though thousands bray around thee!
Yet keep thy zeal in rein; despise
    No gentle preparation;
Flash not God's truth on blinking eyes,
    With reckless inspiration!

Farewell, my brave, my bright-eyed boy!
    And from the halls of learning,
Thy face, my long familiar joy,
    Take, with this friendly warning.
And when with weighty truth thou'rt fraught
    From Life, the earnest preacher,
Think sometimes with a kindly thought
    On me, thy faithful teacher.

AN GOTT.[15]

Vater des Lebens!
Quelle der Wahrheit!
Ziel alles Strebens!
Sonn' aller Klarheit!
Unerreichbarer!
Unbekannter!
Unvergleichbarer!
Unbenannter!
'Lass, O lass dein Lob erschallen
Von dem staunenden Kinderlallen!

Zunge der Deutschen,
Sprache der Denker,
Sei des Gedanken's
Muthiger Lenker!
Zunge der reineren
Geistigen Klarheit,

Sprache der tieferen
Inneren Wahrheit!
Leih' O leih' mir deine Schwinge,
Dass ich das Lob des Hoechsten singe!

Wer will es wagen
Mit strotzenden frechen
Hochtrabenden Worten
Dich auszusprechen?
Wer Dich mit naeselndem
Pfaffen-geklimper,
Dich mit bebluemtem
Dichter-gezimper?
Wer will es wagen
Mit leeren Phrasen,
Mit hohlem Schalle
Froemmelnd zu rasen?
Wer mit Gelehrten
Laut disputiren,
Dich, Wesen der Wesen
Anatomiren?
Ueber Einheiten
Und Dreyeinigkeiten
Mit Lanzen und Schwertern

Ritterlich streiten ?
Wer will mit Priestern
Stuemper Dich nennen,
Der Erde Schoenheit
Frevelnd verkennen ?
Wer will Dich mahlen
Mit Zornes-gebährde
Fluchend die fluechtigen
Kinder der Erde ?
Heiliger ! Heiliger !
Lass mich anbeten,
Furchtsamen Schrittes
Die Schwelle betreten,
Wo meine Mutter
Die ewige LIEBE wohnt,
Wo der Allvater,
Die KRAFT nimmer muede thront !

Du Unbeschreibliche
Ewig Weibliche,[1]

---

[1] *Das Unbeschreibliche*
Hier ist es gethan
Das ewig Weibliche
Zieht uns hinan.—GOETHE, *Faust,* 2ter *Theil.*

Immer werdende,
Neu sich gebaerende,
Heimlich waltende,
Innerlich schaltende,
Frei sich gestaltende,
Wunder-entfaltende,
Du nimmer eilende,
Spielend weilende,
Glueck-vertheilende,
Haltende, heilende,
Reiche NATUR!
Bist Du ein Theil
Des ewig reglichen
Immer beweglichen
Gottes nur?
Oder bist Du
Selbst ein Gott,
Eine Goettinn hehr und heilig?
— Zuegle dich, Zuegle dich!
Wohin so eilig
Bodenlos stuerzt sich
Die nimmer rastende,
Ruchlos hastende,
Frech antastende,

Phantasie?
Das ruhig Seiende,
Schaffend befreiende,
Alles-verbindende,
Endlos sich windende,
Erreichst Du
Mit deinem menschlichen Gruebeln nie!

Vater des Lebens!
Was hab’ ich gethan?
Wie zieht mich, wie zerrt mich
Ein plaudernder Wahn?
Vater des Lebens,
Was hab’ ich gesprochen?
Ich habe die Stille
Der Ehrfurcht gebrochen!
Vater! verzeih’ das freche Spielen;
Nennen wer kann DICH? lehr’ mich Dich
    fuehlen!

ODI PROFANUM VULGUS.

(From Horace.)

Hence ye profane, licentious throngs away!
Cease from ill-omened speech, while I, this day,
    The Muse's priest, shall pour
    A song unheard before,
To youths and spotless maids who own my chastened
    lay.

Kings o'er their subject millions wield the rod;
But kings of kings must quail before the god,
    Whose mighty arm o'erthrew
    The rebel Titan crew,
Great Jove, who shakes sublime Olympus with his
    nod.

This man more forest-belted roods may claim
Than that; one suitor his fair plea will frame

On lineage long and clear,
To win the popular ear;
Another on his life, and pure unspotted name

Will stand; with banded clients at his gate
A third shall force the votes; but soon or late
What comes shall come to all;
One doom to great and small
Shall drop from the deep urn of still-revolving
Fate.

In vain Sicilian dainties goad his tongue
To a forced relish, o'er whose head is hung
The sword by one thin hair;
In vain the birds prepare
Sweet-warbled songs for him; in vain soft lyres are strung
strung

To invite sweet sleep.   Sleep to the labouring man
Comes lightly woo'd, nor scorns the narrow span
That roofs the humble cot;
The shade it scorneth not,
Where Tempe's bosky banks the soft-winged Zephyrs
fan.

Seek thou enough.   The man who seeks no more
Nor turbid Hadria with enchafed roar
      Shall vex, nor, when they rise,
      The Kids, 'mid lowering skies,
Nor when Arcturus' fall brings winter's stormy
    store.

Nor blushing vineyards lashed with angry hail,
Nor cheated hopes when fairest crops shall fail,
      Which or the burning star,
      Or watery power did mar,
When mighty floods rolled down, and swept the corn-
    clad vale.

Vain pride! while with huge piers we block the
    main,
Of straitened homes the finny fish complain;
      There, with his sweating bands,
      The master-mason stands
Urging the work; with him the lord whose high
    disdain

Scorns the dry land.   But though he piles in air
Tower upon tower, pale Fear shall find him there;

Grim Terror shall bestride
The strong-beaked trireme's pride;
Behind the harnessed knight gaunt stalks the spectral
    Care.

If then, nor Phrygian marble, nor the blaze
Of purple brighter than the starry rays,
    Can soothe the sting of woe,
    Nor Persian nard, nor glow
Of bright Falernian wines, where generous Bacchus
    sways;

Why should I pile proud halls with pillars rare,
And modish pomp, to court the envious stare
    Of foolish gazing men?
    Why change my Sabine glen
For wealth that, got with toil, is kept with cumbrous
    care?

BOOK III.

ERATO.

Πᾶς γοῦν ποιητὴς γίγνεται, κἂν ἄμουσος ᾖ τὸ πρὶν, οὗ ἂν Ἔρως ἅψηται.
—PLATO.

Oh Love, the song of life! Oh Love,
The music of the world!

—DOBELL.

THE BOW-WINDOW.

As I came o'er from Patterdale
   To leafy Ambleside,
'Twas there I met the bonnie Scotch lass
   That soon should be my bride.
She sate and looked from a bow-window,
   By the steepy steepy road;
And down upon me, as I passed,
   Her queenly beauty flowed.

I trudged along to Rydal mount,
   I came to green Grasmere,
I sate beside the Poet's grave,
   I looked on the waters clear.
But through the mount, and the mead, and the
      mere
   One sunny presence flowed,

Of the maid that smiled from the bow-window
   At Ambleside on the road.

I wandered up to lone Langdale,
   I clomb the lofty Fell,
And the mist came down, and the storm did bray,
   And the floods did rudely swell.
But through the mist, and the wind, and the rain,
   And the floods that savagely flowed,
That fair face smiled from the bow-window
   At Ambleside on the road.

I turned me back to Ambleside,
   I might no farther wander;
I flung my guide-book in the beck,
   As I tracked its clear meander.
And ever as I nearer came,
   More sweetly round me flowed
That witching smile from the bow-window
   At Ambleside on the road.

I lived a month at Ambleside,
   A month and nearly two,
When hills were green, and streams were small,
   And skies were cloudless blue.

And every night when the westering sun
  With mellowing radiance glowed,
I walked not far from the bow-window
  At Ambleside on the road.

How then from knowing liking grew,
  Let dainty silence cover;
Till Autumn's ripening hour me found
  Her bosom's lord, her lover!
'Twas high in Scandale's ferny glen
  From her lips the sweet words flowed,
That bade me share her bow-window
  At Ambleside on the road.

And now—O Heaven!—what bliss is mine!
  I flung my books away,
My Homer and my Sophocles,
  All papers grim and grey.
For now I've found my nobler self,
  I'm nearer to man and to God,
Since I live on her love in the bow-window
  At Ambleside on the road.

MY LOVE IS LIKE A FLOWERING TREE.

My love is like a flowering tree,
　　Where strength combines with sweetness,
And hard with soft doth well agree,
　　To make one rich completeness !
She's like a peach, whose soft skin fair
　　And mellow pulp containeth
The strong-ribbed, stony kernel, where
　　The vital virtue reigneth.

Meek dovelets I have known and loved,
　　And cooed to their sweet cooing;
Proud eagles, too, I wandering proved,
　　Too high to stoop to wooing.
But she is both—Eagle and Dove—
　　And from her queenly station

Now warms with summer breath of love,
　　Now awes with admiration.

By Heaven! I scarce believe the bliss
　　That I for mine have won her,
The witness of that burning kiss
　　Which stamped my life with honour!
Dear God, if she could look on me,
　　And with her great heart love me,
I'll grow more bold, and henceforth hold
　　No post on Earth above me!

LIKE TO LIKE.

Love me, fair one, love me!
    I bring thee purest love;
Thine own heart would reprove thee,
    Shouldst thou refuse my love.
The God that rules above us,
    Source of life divine,
Who to all good doth move us,
    Framed my heart for thine;
Framed thy heart for mine, love;
    For, since creation's dawn,
By force of law divine, love,
    Like to like is drawn.

Thou seeest how the blossom,
    Many-hued and bright,

Its beauty doth unbosom
  To the glowing light;
How in summer weather
  Birds of kindred wing
In leafy wood together
  Ope their throats, and sing.
So, when with power to win me,
  Thy kindred beauty came,
The smothered love within me
  Rose into a flame!

Then love me, fair one, love me;
  And if thy tongue say, No!
There is a Power above thee
  A wiser way will show.
As step to step, where dancers
  Wheel measured mazes fine,
So to my thought thine answers
  By harmony divine.
For since creation's dawn, love,
  No other law might be,
But like to like is drawn, love,
  As I am drawn to thee!

DORA, HAST THOU EVER SEEN?

Dora, hast thou ever seen
  How, from the sharp sheer-sided mountains,
Down the slopes, so ferny green,
  Sundered flow the twin-born fountains?
To diverse winds their course they take,
  As if to meet no more for ever;
But oft some sudden bend they make,
  And mingled flow, one shining river!

Dora, so my life from thine
  Through long, long years was diverse flowing;
Twin souls were we, but law divine
  Had banned us from the bliss of knowing.

But when His destined day came round,
  Whose will gives law to wind and weather,
Our parted loves swift union found,
  And rushed like two full streams together.

In an instant I was thine,
  And thou wert mine ; no vows we plighted ;
Two halves by mystic law divine
  Were made one whole, when we united.
And I no greater bliss can know
  From God, of all good things the Giver,
Than that our mingled lives may flow
  In love, and truth, and joy for ever !

WHEN A WANDERING ME LISTETH TO GO.

WHEN a wand'ring me listeth to go,
　　Then lists me to wander alone,
To look from an old grey crag,
　　Or muse on an old grey stone.
But, alone if me lists not to go,
　　One only shall wander with me;
And, if her fair name thou wouldst know,
　　Thyself, lovely maiden, art she!
　　　　For thou'rt a part of mine own heart,
　　　　　　And I, when most alone,
　　　　　　Am full of Thee, and my best thoughts
　　　　　　Are less than half my own.

When I sit on an old grey stone,
　　And see the wild roses nod,

So bright, so lucid, so pure,
　　So fresh from the bosom of God,
I look and I love them; for why?
　　'Tis a very small matter, a rose!
But I look with a light from thine eye,
　　And I love but thy bloom in the rose;
　　　　For thou'rt a part, etc.

When I sit on an old green hill,
　　And see the fresh-bickering fountains
Leap forth, and wander at will
　　From the heart of the giant-ribbed mountains!
I love the clear becks as they leap;
　　But who will my fancy condemn,
When I see thy bright thoughts ever keep
　A light-racing bicker with them?
　　　　For thou'rt a part, etc.

When I hear the blithe birds in the wood
　　Their full-souled love-ditties indite,
Making Heaven of green solitude,
　　And thrilling sweet June with delight;
Think I, all the Muses could never
　　Invent fitter measures for me;

For such are the ditties that ever
　　My heart-strings are harping to thee !
　　For thou'rt a part, etc.

Then, maid, if thee listeth to go,
　Me listeth with thee, or alone,
To look from an old grey crag,
　Or to muse on an old grey stone.
But if thou don't love solitudes,
　Then work here at home like a bee,
While I go and bring from the woods
　A bundle of songs made for thee!
　　　　For thou'rt a part of mine own heart,
　　　　And I, when most alone,
　　　　Am full of Thee, and my best thoughts
　　　　Are less than half my own!

LOVELY DORA, HAST THOU SEEN?

Lovely Dora, hast thou seen
  In the land of high-piled mountains,
When in the night a storm hath been,
  A sudden gush of roaring fountains?
Down the gorge, all foaming white,
  The rain-god leaps with rattling quiver,
The rill becomes a beck of might,
  The beck becomes a rolling river.

Dora, so my life did creep
  In the narrow groove of duty,
Till thou didst come with queenly sweep,
  And touched me with the power of beauty.

K

O then my soul gushed out with might,
    A tide of buoyant joy upbore me !
All my thoughts were summer bright,
    All my words were song before thee !

Lovely Dora, thou art gone,
    But dwells with me thy beauteous presence ;
Lives the seed which thou hast sown,
    Germs the thought of joy and pleasance.
For I know thou art not far,
    And the thought of thy great beauty
Turns to music every jar,
    In the dull refrain of duty !

LET ME LOOK INTO THINE EYE!

Let me look into thine eye,
　　Through thine eye into thy soul,
Draw the curtain from the sky,
　　Where the living pictures roll !
I am weary of smooth faces,
　　Looks that play a pretty part,
Shallow smiles and gay grimaces ;
　　Show me, show me, maid, thy heart !

When in gay saloon I found thee
　　Sailing proudly, like a queen,
With an host of fops around thee,
　　Through the fair and flaunting scene :
Sure, I thought, this stately maiden
　　Struts her hour with dainty art,

But behind this masquerading
    Keeps, I'll swear, a guileless heart.

Let me look into thine eye,
    Through thine eye into thy soul,
Of deep thoughts and fancies high
    The living-ciphered book unroll!
I am sick of polished faces,
    Smiles tricked out for fashion's mart;
Worth a thousand practised graces,
    Show me, show me, maid, thy heart!

O BLESSED ATMOSPHERE OF LOVE!

O BLESSED atmosphere of Love,
Thee now I fairly, fully prove!
  For not the balmy spring
More sweet through bursting herb and tree
Breathes genial-pulsing energy,
  Than me thy fragrant wing

Fans constant; O the sweet repose
From iron toils and thorny woes
  On gentle woman's breast!
I will unmail me here. Go, boy,
And make my sword a tinkling toy,
  And with my haughty crest

Brush flies from pleasure's cheek ! I will
The stony-faced and Stoic skill
    To look on blood forbear.
Here, on sweet woman's gentle breast,
Be every sterner sin confessed,
    Thawed every frosty care !

MY FANNY O!

AIR—" *The Lass in yon Town.*"

~~~~~~~~~~~

O WAT ye wha's in yon house,
    Yon stern and stately palace O ?
A forest flower's in yon house,
    Fresh frae the mountain valleys O !
The city dames are nice and prim,
    Tight tied with laces many O ;
But she with love doth freely brim,
    And thinks nae harm, my Fanny O !
O wat ye wha's in yon big house,
    And gars my rhymes sae jingle O ?
A lass—O would I had her crouse
    The queen of my blithe ingle O !
~~~~~~~~~~~

O wat ye wha's in yon house,
    Yon proud and lordly palace O?
Wha would expect in yon house
    The bloom o' mountain valleys O?
Though fairer features I ha'e seen,
    And forms more slender many O;
Yet twa sic frank and friendly een
    I only found in Fanny O!
The learned may mark the lines of art,
    Split nice distinctions many O;
But gi'e thou me the truthful heart,
    The open eye of Fanny O!

Where Beaumont water glides wi' glee
    Frae Cheviot green and grassy O,
There might I wander free wi' thee,
    My blithe, true-hearted lassie O!
O shun the arts of city dames!
    Nae prickly fashion dress thee O!
O sport not thou with fickle flames,
    Nae fopling false caress thee O!
O shun the taint of pride and pelf,
    And, 'mid thy lovers many O,
Choose him who loves the simple self
    Of fresh, free-hearted Fanny O!

FANNY MACMURDOCH.

Fanny MacMurdoch is blithe and bonnie,
　　Fanny MacMurdoch is frank and free;
God bless thee ever, Fanny MacMurdoch,
　　Soothly thou art a joy to see!
Fanny MacMurdoch, Fanny MacMurdoch,
　　Blithe and blooming Fanny MacMurdoch!
My heart was glad, and my heart was sad,
　　When first I looked on Fanny MacMurdoch.

Fanny MacMurdoch is truthful-hearted,
　　Truth she wears in her bonnie blue e'e:
Souls of children, where thou comest,
　　Fanny MacMurdoch, come with thee!

Fanny MacMurdoch, Fanny MacMurdoch,
　　Truthful-hearted Fanny MacMurdoch !
One look I gave, one look I got,
　　And I lost my heart to Fanny MacMurdoch !

O Fanny MacMurdoch, Fanny MacMurdoch,
　　A wicked thought thou gav'st to me ;
I wish I were married twenty times over
　　To thee, and all that's like to thee !
O Fanny MacMurdoch, Fanny MacMurdoch,
　　Blithe, brave-hearted Fanny MacMurdoch,
I'm married already (and can't be divorced)
　　In heart to thee, sweet Fanny MacMurdoch !

O STANEHIVE IS A BONNIE, BONNIE TOUN!

O Stanehive is a bonnie, bonnie toun,
  From its quiet bay bright peeping;
'Twixt the rocks sae hard and bare,
  Like a little Eden sleeping.
There aince lived a bonnie, bonnie lass,
  And worthy was the man wha got her;
She was like the bonnie toun,
  He the rocks of strong Dunottar.

She was mine by rights—ae night
  In the starry clear December,
She did press my hand sae warm,
  Looked sae kindly, I remember.

But for want of needfu' cash,
    I was blate to tell my story;
And sae I lost my bonnie lass,
    And anither cam' afore me.

Truth, she had a laughing e'e,
    And her mou' was made for kissing;
Light her step, and when she spak'
    Ilka word did seem a blessing.
O she was a bonnie, bonnie lass,
    Worthy was the man wha got her;
Ne'er without a tear I pass
    Sweet Stanehive and strong Dunottar!

LOVE'S LULLABY.

Ye waters, wildly pouring,
With hollow murmurs roaring,
Plunging o'er the rocky steep
With a furious foamy sweep,
In the cavern'd caldron boiling,
Turning, tumbling, twisting, toiling,
Sounding from the glen's dark throat
Old hymns of deep and drowsy note;
   Ye waters, hollow-roaring,
   Lull ye, lull my love asleep!

Ye forests, dark-surrounding,
With hollow whispers sounding,

Breath that stirs the horrid woods,
Voice of vasty solitudes,
Like the sea, with murmurs swelling,
Solemn, sacred, awe-compelling,
Speaking to the pious ear
Like God's guardian presence near;
    Ye forests, hollow-sounding,
Lull ye, lull my love asleep!

INVITATION.

Not by Leman's lovely lake,
Or Italy far away,
Where the jocund Sun doth make
Perpetual holiday;
Not in fair and festal Rome,
Or where Venice airy
Piles the palace and the dome
On her waters fairy;
On my own, my Scottish braes,
Where the tall pine darkly sways,
O'er the fresh and purple heather
Green-bedappled with the fern,
Fondly, while we stray together,
I will teach, if thou wilt learn,
To love, sweet maid, to love!

Freshly blows the Autumn breeze
High over Clach-na-Ben,
Fragrant wave the birchen trees
At Dye-brig, low in the glen.
There, if thou with me wilt stray,
Bird in April weather
Never was merrier on the spray
Than we shall be together.
Yes, fair maiden, thou wilt go !
Such sweet silence ne'er meant NO.
Thus my faithful fancy guesses
These bright eyes might ne'er look stern,
And who owns these golden tresses,
She can teach, as well as learn,
To love, sweet maid, to love !

WHEREFORE NOW NOR SONG NOR SONNET ?

Wherefore now nor song nor sonnet
    Write I thee, Eliza dear ?
Love's a plant, the blossom on it
    Rhyme, child of the vernal year :
With the full-grown time it ceases,
Waning as the fruit increases,
    Therefore now nor song nor sonnet
    Write I thee, Eliza dear !

Ever as I would be chiming
    Pretty pointed lines to thee,
Seems a power to rein my rhyming,
    And it reasons thus with me :

L

" Fool, why wilt thou still be prating ?
Truth that's known needs no debating !"
    Therefore I nor song nor sonnet
    Write, Eliza dear, to thee !

I'VE MADE A COVENANT WITH MINE EYES.

I'VE made a covenant with mine eyes
   To meet no more thy glances;
Run he whose hand may seize the prize,
   Whose speed bright Hope enhances!
But me—I'm sold to stern employ;
   I've sworn an oath to Duty,
A soldier's oath; and dare not toy
   With tangling nets of Beauty!

I've looked on thee too long!—thou hast
   A witching spell about thee;
But God hath made me free at last;
   Now I can live without thee!

Let every smooth, soft-bearded boy
    That flits on wings of leisure,
Taste from thy smiles love's dainty joy!
    My work shall be my pleasure.

Then fare thee well!—to grave and gay
    Dispense thy charmèd chalice;
Spread harmless pleasures without pay,
    Sow sweet harm without malice!
But I, whom thou hadst wounded sore,
    The pleasing-painful arrow
Out from my quivering flesh I tore,
    And now am healed from sorrow!

SPORT NOT WITH LOVE!

Sport not with love, if thou art wise;
  Quick from such perilous pastime turn thee!
The light that rays from beauty's eyes
  Shall grow into a flame to burn thee!
If the fair maid may not be thine,
  In feeding love thou feedest sorrow;
One short hour's bliss may make thee pine
  With a life-long wound to-morrow!

'Tis hard, I know, 'tis harsh; but take
  The friendly warning that I bring thee:
This singing bird will turn a snake,
  And in thy bosom sorely sting thee!

When the ripe peaches on the wall
    Are hung too high for thy endeavour,
Even now thy lawless gaze recall,
    Or pine with fruitless greed for ever !

Sport not with love, if thou art wise ;
    Sport not with love !—a spark is pretty ;
But give it breath, and lo ! it flies
    Rampant abroad, and flames a city !
If the fair maid may not be thine,
    From love's luxurious pasture turn thee,
Or these fair eyes that beam benign
    Shall grow a scorching flame to burn thee !

JANET.

I KNOW a lass I will not name,
For in this evil planet
A thousand tongues my praise would blame,
So I'll just call her JANET.
A lass of such fine witching grace,
That, but my sails are furled,
I'd chase her at a rattling pace
For love o'er half the world ;
This dainty Janet!

Hast seen the swan, whose plumes avail
For smoothest luxury's pillow,
That sails and scarcely seems to sail
Full-bosomed o'er the billow :

So graceful she, so stately mild,
  So queenly, so majestic,
Yet sportive as a very child,
  With kindly thoughts domestic,
        This rare young Janet!

Thou know'st the yellow furze in May,
  Its odorous richness flinging
Far o'er brown heath and grassy brae,
  When cuckoo's note is ringing;
So rich in golden gleams is she,
  Such fragrance floateth from her,
It makes me happy as a bee
  Drunk with the breath of Summer
        To look on Janet!

Thou know'st the pure, pellucid lake,
  The mountain stream's fair daughter,
Where tree and tower their image make
  In the soft-cradling water;
So clear, so soft, fair Janet's eye
  Her heart's pure depth discloses,
While eloquent smiles around her fly,
  Like hues from bursting roses,
        So true is Janet!

Nor only true, but seeks for truth
With careful, nice endeavour,
And to this service yields her youth,
With every gift God gave her.
With the strong arms of love she clings
To all Earth's living creatures,
And worships in the meanest things
The trace of God's own features,
This high-souled Janet!

Nor knows alone, but liberal throws
The seeds of truth diffusive,
And with sweet breath away she blows
Each filmy mist delusive.
O what a grace has truth, when she
And such as she are preachers!
To spurn God's law may guiltless be
From harsh and thorny teachers,
But not from Janet!

The Earth is full of lovely things;
Within this teeming planet
To each a separate pleasure springs,
But my delight is JANET.

To ken a star, or gauge a storm,
   Some men will mountains move,
But in my heart the blood grows warm
   When I behold and love
         This rare dear Janet!

DINNA MIND MY GREY HAIRS.

Dinna mind my grey hairs,
  Bonnie, bonnie lady!
My heart is warm and glowing,
  My hand is sure and steady.
But if you'll be mine ain wife,
  My heart's delight, my joy,
You'll find the man with grey hairs
  A young and lusty boy.
      Dinna mind my grey hairs,
        Bonnie, bonnie lady!

Like a goat or antelope
  I can climb a mountain ;
From my brain thoughts bright with hope
  Leap as from a fountain.

I can foot it in a reel
  As light as finch or sparrow,
And often in my heart I feel
  Sweet stings from Cupid's arrow.
        Dinna mind my grey hairs,
          Bonnie, bonnie lady !

Dinna mind my grey hairs,
  Bonnie, bonnie lady !
My blood is coursing freely,
  My wit is quick and ready.
And if you let me circle you
  In love's enraptured arms,
You'll find no youth of twenty-two
  More worthy of your charms.
        Take me with my grey hairs,
          Bonnie, bonnie lady !

JENNY'S SOLILOQUY.

O THAT my braw wooers would study their battle,
   A face of more meekness belike I might show them!
But now they rush on with a reasonless rattle,
   And forget that before we can love we must know
     them.
These hot-bloods, they think that we women are pikes,
   To devour a red rag, or a leaf of white metal;
But a sensible maiden will look ere she likes,
   As a bee smells the flower in the breeze ere it settle.

There's huge-whiskered Harry came swashing from
     town,
   On a pair of stout legs that full bravely did carry
     him;

He thought a red coat with the fair must go down,
  So that very night he besought me to marry him.
Quoth I, I can't tell, you might do very well,
  You have whiskers and legs, and ·your brave name
    is Harry,
But my husband must know me, and Harry must show
    me
  His soul, if he has one, before I can marry!

Then Tommy the student, a smooth-polished man,
  Who soon on his shoulders a surplice will carry,
He thought a good wife should be part of his plan,
  So fresh from his Greek books he asked me to
    marry.
Quoth I, you look sleek, and you're well read in Greek,
  And a logical thrust you can decently parry;
But whether your soul's a man's or a mole's
  I must know, learnèd Tommy, before I can marry!

Next, barrister Bobby came flouncing about,
  As keen as a hawk that will pounce on the quarry;
He thought I must read my Lord Bob on his snout,
  So he said a few smart things, and asked me to
    marry.

Quoth I, that you're clever no man doubted ever,
  With you for an answer no question needs tarry;
But if you claim a part, learnèd sir, in my heart,
  You must show me your own first, then ask me to
    marry!

And so they go bouncing and blundering on,
  The metal before it is hot always striking;
And thus in the end I'll be left quite alone,
  Where no fancy has leisure to grow to a liking.
But of one thing I'm sure, no mate I'll endure,
  Who thinks I can wed his mere beef and his bone;
But he who would win me must first reign within me,
  By the right of a soul, the born lord of my own!

THE BROWN GOWN.

Jenny, what's this?
There's something amiss
About you to-day, though I can't tell what;
'Tis not in the grace
Of your arch-smiling face,
Nor yet in the beautiful bend of your hat.
Yes! now I perceive, you who used to be drest,
Like glorious June in her Sunday vest,
Have doffed your colours, and donned a gown
Of a muddy and meaningless snuffy old brown;
C'est une grande betise, ma chere!

Tell me, did you ever
By lake or by river
See brown primroses prinking the grass?

And wouldn't it be silly,

If rose or lily

Were blooming in brown, when the meadow you pass?

There are flowers of purple, and blue, and gold,

And green is the carpet that covers the mould;

But brown is no blossom, and why should you,

The fairest of flowers, wear so dingy a hue?

C'est une grande betise, ma chere!

For brown is a colour

No hue can be duller;

Brown are green leaves when their glory is fled,

The cold grey stone

Calls the brown moss its own,

And brown is the dust which we fling on the dead.

Brown are the tadpoles in muddy abodes,

Earwigs and beetles, and adders and toads;

But that a fair maid should envelope her charms

In brown, like a Venus in Pluto's grim arms,

C'est une grande betise, ma chere!

Then, Jenny, be wise,

And don't vex my eyes

With a gown of this muddy and meaningless hue;

M

I'd as soon see Apollo
Ride Heaven's blue hollow,
Like a Capuchin monk, or an Old Clothes Jew.
Put on the bright robe, the delight of young Cupid,
When you look so clever, and men look so stupid;
For not even you for a Grace will go down,
When swathed in wide volumes of snuffy old brown.

Laissez donc cette betise, ma chere!

WHO'S THERE, JANET?

Who's there, Janet?—Come and see!
Come to the window, and peep with me!
Look from the window, my dainty fair,
I'll show you a sight that's somewhat rare.
What you sought, since first you began
To be a woman, I'll show you—a man;
A man complete in body and soul,
With every part that builds up a whole.
There he stands, and leans on the wall,
So firm, so strong, so noble, so tall.
He looks on the village; he's rapt in the view—
Or thinking, it may be, on something like you.
Mark him, Jenny, and measure him well!
  Who knows what may yet be true?
He's a perfect man, every inch of the ell,
  And made perhaps, just made for you!

None of your perking, critical fops,

Who go sniffling about the booksellers' shops,

Smelling each work before publication,

That they may give an account to the nation.

Fellows who write in the weekly Reviews,

With all men for their theme, and themselves

    for their Muse,

Swaying with large, unfettered dominion

The rambling realms of babbled opinion,

Hanging this sign from the tip of their nose :

" *Ready to meet whate'er you propose*

In the shape of a YES *with a legion of* NOES !"

Men so clever the world yet never

    Beheld their like, since the sophists of old

Did Socrates wise to death deliver

    For speaking plain truth with raillery bold.

Men who are ever strutting about

With ready-made judgments on their snout,

Who nothing in Heaven or Earth revere,

But think God made all things for a sneer ;

On faults of their betters who daintily feed,

As flies on ordure feast with greed,

Thinking the readiest way for the small

To grow great, is by lopping the heads of the tall.

And weening they've turned—O wonderful
    men !
The balance of fate by a snip of their pen ;
Forgetting that they, infallible guides,
Themselves are only a straw on the tides,
And, when they are wisest, direct the people,
Just as the weather-cock does on the steeple !

Who's there, Janet ?—Come and see !
Come to the window, and peep with me !
Look from the window, my dainty fair,
I'll show you a sight that's somewhat rare.
What you sought, since first you began
To be a woman, I'll show you—a man ;
A man complete in body and soul,
With every part that builds up a whole.
There he stands, and leans on the wall,
So firm, so strong, so noble, so tall.
He looks on the village ; he's rapt in the view,
Or thinking, it may be, on something like you.
Mark him, Jenny, and measure him well !
    Who knows what may yet be true ?
He's a perfect man, every inch of the ell,
    And made, perhaps, just made for you.

None of your butter-lipped clerical fops,
All decently drilled in Tutorial shops
Of Oxford and Cambridge, so proper and prim,
With orthodox sentences crammed to the brim.

Men who have eyes, but who never can look
Beyond what their fathers for oracles took,
But through sense and through nonsense will
    swear to a book.

Greeklings well-furnished with learnèd quota-
    tion,
To vamp an address, or patch an oration,
Who lisp in elegant verse or prose
What no one cares for, and every one knows,
And think all common-places uncommonly
    clever,
If them but a Greek or a Roman deliver.

Men who patter their collects and creeds
As glibly as Papists number their beads,
Who with cross and candle, and cassock and
    cope,
Help women and weaklings half-way to the
    Pope,
And send a palsied old Duke or Duchess
Limping to Heaven on priestly crutches;

For such is the nature of man, he would fain
Work out his faith, but it bothers his brain :
So he hires a priest to think for him,
Who prinks out a creed all decent and trim,
That tickles his fancy and suits his whim ;
And so by this subtle device we inherit
A charter of quibbles, and count it a merit.
Of briars and brambles a bundle we cherish,
And fret if a single prickle may perish,
Till by hallowing time and long veneration
Sheer nonsense becomes the sole sense of the
        nation.
These are the men who make nonsense appear
As proper as sense with logic so clear,
You can't but think it a sin and a treason
In matters so sacred to trust to your reason.
You see the advantage of going to school,
You can't but be right when you argue by rule :
From erudite lips, so polite and so civil,
Nought sounds in the pulpit more sweetly than
        drivel.

Who's there, Janet ?—Come and see !
Come to the window, and peep with me !

Look from the window, my dainty fair,

I'll show you a sight that's somewhat rare ;

What you sought since first you began

To be a woman, I'll show you—a man :

A man complete in body and soul,

With every part that builds up a whole.

There he stands, and leans on the wall,

So firm, so strong, so noble, so tall !

He looks on the village ; he's rapt in the view,

Or thinking, it may be, on something like you.

Mark him, Jenny, and measure him well !

   Who knows what may yet be true ?

He's a perfect man, every inch of the ell,

   And made, perhaps, just made for you !

      None of your moody, poetical fops,

      Who mingle their honey with gall and hops,

      Fumes of tobacco, and opiate drops.

      Men who think all things here out of joint,

      But God did to them this mission appoint,

      To dream broad-eyed for a day and a night,

      And maunder an Epos to set it all right,

      And beget upon clouds a new generation

      After their likeness, to model the nation.

      These are the men whose heart is broken,

      God knows how—but their verse is the token

Who, because they do not find
All things on Earth just made to their mind,
Because the breeze will sometimes blow
Just in their teeth, where they mean to go ;
Because a rose has ever a thorn,
And dark clouds oft obscure the morn ;
Or because in a shadowless land
A tree won't grow at the word of command ;
And an old house of course must stand,
Till a new one is raised by the builder's
    hand ;
Or because a sheep must die,
Before they can feast on a mutton-pie,
Or because a fair girl with a jaunty bonnet
Won't fetch a sigh, when they whimper a sonnet ;
Straightway swell with oracular rage,
And blot with bile their fretful page,
And in this beautiful world can see
Nothing but mildew and misery ;
Who, when the birds in spring are singing,
And all the woods with joy are ringing,
Sit chiming creation's funeral knell,
And say that the Earth is a seething hell,
Where only devils and dunces dwell,

    Where a thousand fools are led by a knave,
    And the proudest is ever the foremost slave,
    Where a prize to the clown and the flunkey
        falls,
    But the Jove-born poet must sing to the walls!

Who's there, Janet?—Come and see!
Come to the window, and peep with me!
Look from the window, my dainty fair,
I'll show you a sight that's somewhat rare;
What you sought since first you began
To be a woman, I'll show you—a man:
A man complete in body and soul,
With every part that builds up a whole.
Clear to see, and quick to discern,
With a child-like eye ever looking to learn;
With a heart where fervid oceans flow,
A firm set will, and a sure-poised blow.
This is a man whose wit never strands
   On shores forbid to human intruding,
Nor wildly grasps with violent hands
   A mist, which he mistakes for a pudding.
You'll never find him choking with books
   The fire within which freely glows,

Nor fumbling in distant library nooks
  For what lies plainly before his nose.
This is a man who leaves a trace,
Where he plants his foot, that none may efface.
He looks with wary consideration,
  Measures his ground, and ponders his plan ;
But, when he once has taken his station,
  Is true to his thought as a chief to his clan.
This is a man whose eye discerns
  What each thing means in the scheme of Nature,
Who wisely follows and lovingly learns,
  Each linked to each by the great Creator.
In a star, or a tree, or a stone,
  He sees the secret virtue lurking ;
All things good he calls his own,
  And all rejoice to acknowledge his working.
Plant him on a broad, bare hill,
  To-morrow the grass will there be growing !
Give him a sandy waste to till,
  To-morrow the brook will there be flowing !
Make him lord of a wildered parish,
Where all the people are rude and bearish,
He'll build a church, he'll build a school,
And teach each workman to wield his tool.

And, if you oppose him in anything good,

He'll march right on with a conquering mood,

Knowing that fools are fuel and food,

By natural destiny made for the wise,

To feed the flame of their victories.

I've told you his type.   What things he has done,

What famous battles he hath won,

Bloody and bloodless, at home and abroad,

Like Paul, a fellow-worker with God,

You'll hear from himself, I hope, very soon.

He means to be here all the month of June ;

And if you and he don't come together,

I am no judge of wind and weather.

He was one of the first who began

The close death-grapple at Inkermann ;

(You see the medal he worthily wears,

Though many a snob that honour shares).

When he came home and sheathed his sword,

By an uncle's death he was made the lord

Of a magnificent Highland estate,

   Worth some five or six thousand a-year,

Where he lives on his property—strange to relate—

   And cares much more for the men than the deer.

And now he leads the happiest life,

And wants but one thing—that's a wife,

Not quite unworthy of himself ;
For he won't marry for blood or pelf,
Or ev'n for the grace—enough for many—
Of a fair face without a penny ;
But he wants a woman whose soul gives a tone
The natural concord of his own.
So he told me.   I said there are few
Pitched on the same high key with you ;
But I know one who, I think, will do.
And now, my dear Jenny, I've told you all.
You may study him still where he leans on the wall,
So firm, so strong, so noble, so tall.
He looks on the village ; he's rapt in the view,
Or thinking, it may be, on something like you.
Mark him, Jenny, and measure him well !
  Who knows what may yet be true ?
He's a perfect man, every inch of the ell,
  And made, I'll swear, just made for you.

THE METAMORPHOSIS OF PLANTS.[16]

(From the German of Goethe.)

WHY should it be, thou ask'st me well, so fair but to
    confound,
This garden rich, that spreads it breadth of broidered
    beauty round?
Names, learnèd names, thou hear'st, a host; a barbar-
    ous-sounding train
They march, but still, as one comes in, the other leaves
    the brain.
And yet, belovèd, 'tis one truth, not complex, not
    profound,
One sacred simple truth, that rules this maze of tangled
    sound :

The ever-varying flowery forms, their thousands are
    but one;
There is a law that's like in all, but quite the same in
    none.
O! my heart's chosen, if the thought that subtly stirs
    the brain,
Can teach the tongue, I'll tell thee now this law, nor
    tell in vain.
Behold the plant, by what nice rule, from the dark-
    groping root
Step after step it mounts the scale to blossom bright
    and fruit.
Behold the seed, the little seed, with silent plastic
    might,
How nurturing Earth the case unfolds, and to the
    genial light,
The ever-moving holy light, the delicate frame com-
    mends,
The slight, thin, leafy frame, that soon to gorgeous
    height ascends.
Simple the power slept in the seed; a nascent type is
    there
Of all that shall be, nicely wrapt, and swathed with
    curious care;

Half-formed and colourless, root and stem, leaflet and
      leaf there slept,
Their charmèd life all safe from harm by the arid
      kernel kept,
Till gentle dews and genial rain forth-draw the swell-
      ing might,
That shoots elastic from its bed of circumambient
      night.
But simple still the primal shoot; as in the boy the
      man,
Here lies of the full tree immense, the unexpanded
      plan.
But mark, anon an impulse new, knot tower'd on knot
      behold!
And still as higher mounts the stalk, the primal type
      unrolled
Repeats itself; like, not the same; for in the leafy
      show
The upper floats with ampler pride than that which
      grew below.
More deeply cut, and cleft, and carved, and fringed
      in various trim,
The parts dispread, once closely-twined in the in-
      ferior limb.

Thus step by step the growth proceeds, till perfect on
the view
It bursts, a wonder ever old, a wonder ever new;
So giant-ribbed, so straggling free, in swelling breadth
dilated,
As Nature's self were weak to check the impulse she
created.
But she is wise; and reining here the pride o' the leafy
veins,
Gently prepares the higher change, where perfect
beauty reigns;
In narrower cells with milder pulse and calmer flow
she lingers,
And soon the delicate frame displays the working of
her fingers.
Back from the broad and leafy fringe the keen pulsa-
tion flows,
And buoyant now the topmost stem more light and
graceful grows;
Leafless the tender stalklet's grace shoots eagerly on
high,
And soon a shape of wonder bursts, and fills the
studious eye.

Leaflet with leaflet trimly paired, the counted, the
	untold,
Rise, and, with nice adjustment ranged, their spread-
	ing wings unfold.
The parted cup unbinds its charge, and free in
	sunny ray
The million-coloured crowns aloft their blushing
	wealth display.
Thus Nature triumphs in her work, and in full glory
	shows
Each step i' the measured scale, through which to such
	fair height she rose ;
And wonder still detains the eye, oft as the breeze-
	stirred blossom,
On delicate stalklet perched sublime, nods o'er the
	leafy bosom.
But not this gorgeous wealth remains : the strong
	creative power
Lives in the core ; the hand divine stirreth the con-
	scious flower,
And lo ! with inward-curling force, each fine and
	slender thread
Elastic springs to find its mate, and with its like to
	wed :

And now they meet, the lovely pairs, and by a law
  divine,
In nuptial rings they stand around the consecrated
  shrine,
While Hymen hovers near, and wanton breezes
  odorous blow,
And clouds of genial dust forth roll, and vital fountains flow.
Asunder now, and cased apart, stands every swelling
  germ,
Soft-bosomed in the pulpy fruit, that shields its growth
  from harm;
And Nature here the circle ends of her eternal working,
But still within the old the seed of a new life is lurking.
Link unto link she adds; that thus, as countless ages
  roll,
Part after part may share the pulse that stirs the
  mighty whole.
Look now, belovèd, on this web of broidered beauty
  round,
And feel it ne'er was woven thus so fair but to confound.

Each leafy plant thou see'st declares the never chang-
    ing laws,
And every flower, loud and more loud, proclaims the
    Eternal Cause.
'Nor here alone: once recognised the Godhead's
    mystic trace,
Thou'lt see through each most strange disguise the
    now familiar face;
In creeping grub, in wingèd moth, in various man
    thou'lt know
The one great soul that breathes beneath the curious-
    shifting show.
Bethink thee, then, how, in the hours that first to-
    gether drew
Our hearts, from light acquaintance' germ familiar
    converse grew,
From converse sweet by gentle change how potent
    friendship rose,
Till perfect love within our breasts both flower and
    fruitage shows.
And this, bethink, what woven web of blest emotions
    grew,
Phase after phase of various love, the same but ever
    new!

And learn to enjoy the hour! pure love still upward
strives to float
To that high sphere where wish to wish, and thought
responds to thought,
Where feeling blent with feeling, raptures thrilled
with raptures rare,
In bonds of a diviner life, unite the blissful pair.

BOOK IV.

EUTERPE.

The Muse, nae poet ever fand her,
Till by himsel' he learned to wander,
Adown some trotting burn's meander,
      And no think lang;
O sweet to stray, and pensive ponder
      The heart-felt sang!

—BURNS.

Le bon Dieu me dit, chante,
Chante, pauvre petit !

—BERANGER.

MY VOCATION.

Through life I went blundering on,
　　Trying this thing and that for employ;
But of trades and professions was none
　　Would suit such a cross-witted boy.
One day, when I strayed through the wood,
All dark and despairing of good,
I heard a sweet bird on the spray,
And thus it seemed chirping to say—
" Why don't you try to sing, sing,
Cheerily, cheerily, poor little thing ? "

Of theology, warranted sound,
　　I made a devout navigation,
But the bigots soon ran me aground,
　　With sulphurous blasts of damnation.

Besides, I soon found that God's plan
Was too vast for the small wit of man ;
So I took the sweet hint from the spray,
And my heart with the bird 'gan to say—
" Love man and his Maker, and sing, sing,
Piously, piously, poor little thing !"

I served with a lawyer some time,
　　And I used the lithe trick of the jaw,
But to me all their speeches sublime
　　Seemed very like thrashing of straw.
With words very deftly they wrangled,
But the sense in the scuffle was strangled ;
So I went to the bird on the spray,
And my heart with its song seemed to say—
" Leave wrangling and jangling, and sing, sing,
Peacefully, peacefully, poor little thing !"

To combat the worst of our foes,
　　With the Doctors I then did embark ;
The disease they were quick to expose,
　　But the cure was to guess in the dark.
So, being no friend of humbug,
I threw away lancet and drug ;

And I went to the bird on the spray,
And my heart with its song seemed to say—
" The best of all cures is to sing, sing,
Hopefully, hopefully, poor little thing !"

And now I'm a minstrel by trade,
    And though I don't gather much money,
Since the time when that bird I obeyed,
    My heart is a flower full of honey.
From grim theological doctors,
From lawyers and drug-concoctors,
I'm free as a bird on the spray;
And a voice in my heart still doth say—
" Thy wisdom below is to sing, sing,
Fearlessly, fearlessly, poor little thing !"

MY WISH: AN IDYLL.

"Tell me thy wish!"—Though wishes are foolish,
    yet sometimes a friend may
Speak to a friend the thought, that in the back-
    ground of his fancy
Floats serenely, remote from the urgent spur of the
    moment.
When my battle is fought—for I would live as a
    soldier,
Gallantly shaping my life to the type of a noble con-
    ception,
Fighting with faithless hearts, and brains of no specu-
    lation,
Meagre formalists, men who swear by statute and
    parchment,

Clogging with blocks from the past the glorious march
    of the future :—
But when my Malakoff falls—or I am maimed in
    the storming—
Then I know the spot, where I would build me a cot-
    tage,
Neat and trim, with lancet-windows quaint, and a
    bulging
Bow to the West, a porch to the South with stiff
    old ivy
Roofed, and flanked on each side by a trellised veran-
    dah, bound with
Roses and Traveller's Joy. Remote it lies in a mea-
    dow,
Where the river, the son of the mountain, before with
    the briny
Billow he mingles, around the base of the wooded
    enclosure
Rushes with circular sweep, and leaves a plain in the
    middle.
Silently then he gathers his strength, and sombrely
    winding
Through a deep, dark chasm, is lost in the eddies of
    ocean.

Here my cottage shall stand; and here, before my
    window,
Densely massed shall the sycamore spread its bounti-
    ful shadow
Over the daisied green, where the mill-stream winding .
    clearly
Circles me round with peace, and the twin-spired
    hoary cathedral
Peeps through the trees. Here I, with my wife, my
    faithful companion,
Lovingly quick to my faults, and jealously keen for
    my honour,
Wisely would cherish the years that ripen the spirit
    for glory.
Here, with a bevy of bright-eyed boys—my own or
    my sister's—
I in the morning will rise, and sow the peas in the
    garden,
Trim the hedges, or bind the rasps, or dig the
    potatoes.
Here, in the heat of the day, my leisure shall know
    me, my study,
Painted with dancing Graces, Mercuries, Pans, and
    Apollos,

Shelved with books, and piled with papers of youth-
    ful remembrance.

O ! the luxury then to take my Foulis' Homer,

Gift of Forbes, my friend, and spread before me its
    ample

Large-typed beautiful page, and spout the wrath of
    Achilles

Loud with rhythmical chaunt, as often in youthful
    fervour

I, on the breezy brow of Morven or mighty Muicdhui,

Shouted my Greek to the winds ! or, should my
    humour be thoughtful,

Then in my ear shall sound the melodious wisdom of
    Plato,

Deep-mouthed, voicing the things that remain, when
    the pride of the Present

Passes, and God is felt, the centre of deathless
    Being :

Or, if the comical whim shall tickle my diaphragm,
    lightly

Thou, Aristophanes then, with lusty humour redun-
    dant,

Shaking thy blossoms of wit, like flowers in summer,
    shalt cheer me.

Thus I'll muse o'er my books, till the slanting beam
    in the window
Shows the sun half-way from his noon-day height to
    his setting.
Then my faithful companion, my wife, with loving
    inquiry,
Taps at my door, and a bevy of bright-eyed boys up-
    roarious
Rushes behind.   Abroad we sally, and carelessly
    wander
Over the fields, or across the deep stream paddle the
    wherry :
Many a flower we pluck, and many a fern from the
    shaded
Root of the old grey crag, and with learnèd phrase
    botanical
Daisy and crow-foot baptize, and the crimp-leaved
    blue-flowered speedwell ;
Stamens and pistils we count, and talk of loves and
    marriages
Mystical-typed by God in the life of the leafy crea-
    tion.
Then my faithful companion, my wife, with thoughts
    of affection,

Thinks of the poor and the sick. We visit the old
    schoolmaster,
Call on the gardener's widow, and talk of her son,
    who so bravely
Scaled the heights, and spiked the guns at glorious
    Alma ;
Leave a book for Tommy, the learnèd son of the
    ploughman,
Who, his mother hath said, shall mount the pulpit,
    and, one day,
Stir the hearts of the people, and thunder, as Guthrie
    thunders.
Thus we roam till the westering sun with lengthening
    shadow
Falls ; and then return to the sound of the gong for
    dinner.
Now to dinner we go—my dinner shall never be
    lonely—
Me the minister, clerk of the Church by law esta-
    blished,
Me the Dissenter shall know ; one liberal board re-
    ceives them.
Hock and Claret shall whelm the sectarian hate in
    their bosoms,

Drowned in mellow delight. Likewise the village
    physician
I to my table will call, and every man whom the parish
Honours, for virtue, or knowledge, or public spirit
    reputed.
We with various talk will season the generous flowing
Soul-discumbering wine—the battles of Tory and
    Whig men,
Church and State, the Russian's wile, and the Prus-
    sian's weakness,
Freedom down-trampled in France, and Popery
    nursled in Oxford:
Science, religion, and art, theology, heresy, schism,
Records of God in the rock, huge antediluvian reptiles,
Mummied in beds of stone, with fishes and crabs
    gigantic;
Maurice, and Lewis, and Kingsley, Macleod the
    jocund apostle,
Thackeray, Dickens, and Browning, and Carlyle, king
    of the Titans;
Hamilton, Hegel, and Kant, the Infinite and the In-
    soluble,
Harsh-grained bigots at home, and cloud-brained
    mystics in Deutschland.

Thus shall flow the discourse : the gentlemen then to
    the parlour
Ripely retire ; and there, with the clatter of saucers
    and tea-cups,
Rattling dice, and thoughtful chess, and whist four-
    handed,
Critical talk with the ladies of Tennyson's Idylls and
    Balder,
Adam Bede, and Miss Muloch, Macaulay, Massey,
    and Aytoun,
Sermons at home and abroad, the fiery bray of the
    unkempt
Gospelling Scot, and the smooth-lipped polish of gen-
    tleman priests, who
Guide with innocuous grace the Cockney's silken
    devotions,
Lightly the hour we beguile. Or, if the Squire's
    son, the lieutenant,
Fresh from India, gaping about for a wife and a
    fortune,
Deigns to know my roof, then he with the Doctor's
    daughter
Lightly shall wheel the graceful waltz, or through
    the mettlesome

Reel shall merrily tramp.   Or Mary, the sunny-faced
    maiden,
Eldest born of the Free Church minister, beautiful
    Mary,
She at the landlord's call shall warble an old Scotch
    ballad,
Banks o' Doon, or Auld Langsyne, or Wandering
    Willie ;
Or with a graver Muse shall lift the note of devotion,
Angels bright and fair, thy jubilant pæan, St
    Asaph,
Luther's hymn, or the prayer that Kœrnér prayed in
    the battle.
Then my faithful companion, my wife, with godly
    remembrance,
Goes to the minister, clerk to the Church by law
    established,
Whispers a word, and brings from the shelf the big
    old Bible.
He unclaspeth the book, and gravely readeth a chapter,
Weighty with wisdom of love, and consolation, and
    warning.
Then he bendeth his knee, and prays to the mighty
    Creator ;

We with him give thanks to the bountiful Giver of
  all things,
Gratefully reckon the joys of the day, and with pious
  assurance
Find in the fruits of the Past the germ that pledges
  the Future.

Here thou hast it, my friend: the wish of my heart
  is spoken;
Wish not uttered before, and scarcely thought: for,
  believe me,
Wishes belong not to man, but what God sends with
  a manly
Courage to welcome, and firmly to grasp the good of
  the moment.

THE WEE HERD LADDIE.[17]

Little Andrew, lively Andrew,
   Herding of the kine,
Looking 'neath thy curly locks
   Wi' bright and merry eyne!
Stretched upon a furzy brae,
   Wi' bonnet, plaid, and crook,
What should a wee herd laddie do
   Wi' a Greek and Latin book?

There's mony a thought in Andrew's head;
   His fancy freely wanders
North and South, and East and West,
   And still he reads and ponders.
There's something brewing in his brain;
   Beneath his plain grey plaidie,

Adventures beat in every vein
  O' the wee bare-footed laddie.

And what's become of Andrew now ?
  I hear he's gone to college ;
He saved a penny in the hills,
  To pay his fees of knowledge.
And Andrew now is Doctor hight,
  And now the leech is gone,
To serve their need who bravely bleed
  In Spain with Wellington.

And Andrew's now a man of proof .
  At sacred Duty's call
Brave Andrew never stands aloof ;
  On him hang great and small.
And now he's come from Waterloo,
  Wi' the Duke that ruled the wars,
And they, who know his service true,
  Have gemmed his breast wi' stars.

And now he's grown a belted knight,
  The wee bare-footed laddie,
Wi' heart as pure and eye as bright
  As when he wore the plaidie.

The mightiest Duke in a' the land
  Who scorns a wee herd laddie,
Now shakes " Sir Andrew" by the hand—
  The knight that wore the plaidie !

THE OLD SOLDIER OF THE GARELOCH HEAD.

I've wander'd east and west,
   And a soldier I hae been;
The scars upon my breast
   Tell the wars that I have seen.
But now I'm old and worn,
   And my locks are thinly spread,
And I'm come to die in peace,
   By the Gareloch Head.

When I was young and strong,
   Oft a wandering I would go,
By the rough shores of Loch Long,
   Up to lone Glencroe.
But now I'm fain to rest,
   And my resting-place I've made,

On the green and gentle bosom
    Of the Gareloch Head.

'Twas here my Jeanie grew,
    Like a lamb amid the flocks,
With her eyes of bonnie blue,
    And her gowden locks.
And here we often met,
    When with lightsome foot we sped,
O'er the green and grassy knolls,
    At the Gareloch Head.

'Twas here she pined and died—
    O! the salt tear in my e'e
Forbids my heart to hide
    What Jeanie was to me!
'Twas here my Jeanie died,
    And they scoop'd her lowly bed,
'Neath the green and grassy turf,
    At the Gareloch Head.

Like a leaf in leafy June,
    From the leafy forest torn,
She fell; and I'll fall soon,
    Like a sheaf of yellow corn.

For I'm sere and weary now,
    And I soon shall make my bed
With my Jeanie, 'neath the turf
    At the Gareloch Head.

MAY SONG.

O'ER the brown heath far, by the steep red scaur,
 Where the yellow furze bloom is glowing;
When the keen cold East, and the North hath ceased,
 And the soft-winged South is blowing;
  Away! away! away!
  Where bright shines the May,
And the fields are green with growing!

Where the dark old pine, in the bright sunshine,
 Its fresh green tips is trimming;
Where the light feathered throng, with the airy song
 Of full-throated glee are brimming;
  Away! away! away!
  The lusty May
Let us with them be hymning!

Where the bright blue sky, on the pinnacle high
  Of dark Lochnagar, rests clearly;
Where snows no more wreathe the frontlets hoar
  Of bleak Ben-Awn[1] so drearly;
      Away! away! away!
      Hymn the lusty May,
Where the streams are bickering cheerly!

Like a ruddy-faced boy, with a vagabond joy,
  When the long school term is over;
Like a bright-haired girl, with a light-tossed curl,
  When she runs to meet her lover;
      Away! away! away!
      So may the lusty May
Still find me a lusty rover!

[1] Written as pronounced, but properly spelled *Avon*.

POUR FORTH THE WINE.

Pour forth the wine, the ruby wine!
And with thine eye look into mine,
    Thou friend of olden days!
Heap up the blazing logs!   Not here
On this grey ridge of granite drear,
Boon April spends her flowery cheer,
    To wake the poet's lays.
The East wind through the ungenial day
    Blows meagre, thin, and chill,
And laggard Winter's freezing ray
    Gleams from the snow-patched hill.

Pour forth the wine, the ruby wine!
And with thine eye look into mine,
    Thou friend of olden days!

Cheer me with love and truth : for I
Oft seek in vain, beneath the sky,
The true heart, from the open eye
    That looks with guileless gaze.
A cold and caution-crusted race
  Here fans few joys in me ;
But when I see a clear, bright face,
  I flourish, and am free !

Pour forth the wine, the ruby wine !
And with thine eye look into mine,
    Thou friend of olden days !
Speak of devotion's fiery breath,
Friendship and love more strong than death.
And high resolve, and manly faith,
    That walks in open ways.
Look as thou didst long years ago,
  And read my heart with thine,
That love and truth may freely flow.
    To bless the ruby wine !

‘A SONG OF GLEN LUI BEG.’[18]

O THE rare old pines of Glen Lui!
  With a shout I hailed them then,
When first to the high Muichdhui
  I clomb, through the wild mountain glen.
    But where be the men that should people the
      glen ?
    Where be the kilted brave Highlandmen ?
    The men, to their king and their country true,
    Who stood like a wall at red Waterloo,
      And, with firm-rooted spears,
      Checked the mailed cuirassiers,
    When thrice to the charge, like a tempest, they
      flew ?
    O where is the cot, with its smoke curling blue
    Through the rare old pines of Glen Lui ?

O the rare old pines of Glen Lui!
  Right blithely I greeted them then,
When I whistled my way to Muichdhui,
  Through the folds of the green-winding glen.
    But where be the men that should people the
      glen?
    Woe's me for the kilted brave Highlandmen!
    Banished they live from their dear native shore,
    Beyond the Atlantic's broad billowy roar;
      For the Law hath a care
      Of a stag and a hare,
    And the red grouse that whirrs o'er the measure-
      less moor;
    But the cottar it drives to a far foreign shore,
    From his home 'mid the pines of Glen Lui!

AUSTRALIAN EMIGRANT'S SONG.

(GERMAN BURSCHEN AIR—*So nimmt ihn hin, etc.*)

THEN fare thee well, thou land of Whig and Tory,
Thou home of gold and glory,
Thou famous British land, farewell!
God knows the truth, I love thee well;
But, since thou hast no place for me,
I'll show no peevish face to thee;
I'll seek a home in NEW SOUTH WALES.

The world is wide: Hope is a gallant rider;
God is a good provider:
Faith's portion he appointeth sure.
Farewell, my Scottish mount and moor!

Where summer smiles more cheerily,
Nor winter frowns so drearily;
I'll find a home in NEW SOUTH WALES.

Farewell, dim nooks ! ye dark and dingy gables !
Ye ancient inky tables,
Where many a peaking penman pines,
Where never blessed sun-light shines !
The bullock I'll be chasing now,
Right stoutly I'll be racing now
O'er hill and dale, in NEW SOUTH WALES.

GOD save thee well, thou hectic and full-blooded,
With millions overflooded,
Where labour ill redeems from want,
And giant weeds in purple flaunt !
The healthy, brawny arm alone
Is king, work is the charm alone,
To bind the gods, in NEW SOUTH WALES.

God heal thy strifes, thou land of partisanship,
Of narrow caste and clanship,
Where Nature shrinks from Fashion's ban,
And all has rights, save only MAN !

No close noblesse shall class me now,
No haughty Church harass me now,
Where life is free in NEW SOUTH WALES.

Then fare thee well, thou land of Whig and Tory!
Thou home of gold and glory!
Nor gold nor glory gav'st thou me;
Yet not with cursing leave I thee.
While here ye fight your quarrels out,
My soul its free song carols out
To wood and wold, in NEW SOUTH WALES.

WORK AWAY.[19]

YE toiled ones who sigh for the down and the roses,
 While ye march to the beat of the drum,
And deem that, when life's measured drudgery closes,
 A long taskless Sabbath shall come ;
  I tell ye, in vain
  Ye sigh and complain,
The disease and the cure are both whims of the brain:
 All things by deep labour are stirred ;
Work away!   Work away!   Work away!
 So cries the American bird.

The flower-bulb may rest when dull Winter it beareth,
 But when Spring comes, and bright sunny sheen,
When the many-hued flower, and ripe fruit it pre-
  pareth,
 It toils then unceasing, I ween.

For no rest Nature knows,
Where the heart warm glows,
And in mystical currents the strong tide flows ;
With our labour our life is interred.
Work away !   Work away !   Work away !
So cries the American bird.

In vain would ye break, with a fretful revulsion,
The force that subdues soul to soul ;
Each power on the other a kindly compulsion
Imposes, to perfect the whole.
In his march Old Time,
If you will not climb,
Will leave you to gather the fruit of your crime ;
Whoso will not spur must be spurred.
Work away !   Work away !   Work away !
So cries the American bird.

Leave ease to the idols of old Epicurus ;
Through danger, and doubt, and delay,
To the word of the truth with strong faith we will
moor us,
And work, while 'tis called to-day ;
For God no repose
In the wide world knows,

But working and weaving His wise Spirit goes,
   And the voice of his preaching is heard,
Work away!   *Work away!*   *Work away!*
   In the warning American bird.

POOR CROW.

As I came through the garden ground,
　　I met a little crow,
With short-clipt wing, in narrow bound,
　　Hobbling, hobbling low.
Who clipt thy wing, thou little crow?
　　I wish that wight may die!
'Tis seemly when worms creeping go,
　　But birds were made to fly,
　　　　　　Poor crow!

Who's like to thee?—A bard, whose thought
　　Once spanned the welkin wide,
But now he drags a heavy boat,
　　Against life's muddy tide.

Who's like to thee?—A king high-thron'd,
  Who ruled from sea to sea,
But homeless now, an outcast thing,
  He creeps o'er Earth like thee,
        Poor crow!

Then take my pity for thy plight,
  Thou poor misfortuned thing,
And love me, while I hate the wight
  Who clipt thy venturous wing.
So long thou hoppest on my rood,
  Thou hast a friend in me,
And while I feed on mortal food,
  I'll keep a crumb for thee,
        Poor crow!

THE CRICKET ON THE TREE.[20]

As I came up from Marathon,
  To high Pentelico,
I heard a cricket on a tree
  Singing just so :
Birry—birr—wirr—burr—wurr !
  Cricket on a tree !
From morn to night, in sunny light,
  With mirth and jollity !
        Birry—birr—wirr—burr—wurr !
          Cricket on a tree !
          Burr—wurr—birr— wirr !
          What could more happy be ?

Quoth I, thou airy little thing,
  I much would like to know,

Why from thy throat, or from thy wing,
  The sweet song whirreth so ?
Birry—birr—wirr—burr—wurr !
  Cricket on a tree,
A merry spright, from morn to night,
  Thou singest pleasantly.
        Birry—birr—wirr, etc.

Then spake to me that airy thing,
  Thou mortal, toiling low,
Who hath not heard, both beast and bird,
  That man was born to woe ?
Birry—birr—wirr—burr—wurr !
  The truth I tell to thee,
I sing because I'm not a man,
  But a cricket on a tree !
        Birry—birr—wirr, etc.

Quoth I, thou cricket sage and sweet,
  Men fret and fume, I know,
But I'm a minstrel to my trade,
  And let contention go.
Birry—birr—wirr—burr—wurr !
  Cricket on a tree !

There's one on earth that shares thy mirth,
　　The bard is kin to thee !
　　　　Birry—birr—wirr, etc.

The cricket spake—If thou art wise,
　　Above the human rabble,
I'll shelter thee, beneath my tree,
　　From each unholy squabble.
Birry—birr—wirr—burr—wurr !
　　Poet, turn and flee
From Church and State, in high debate,
　　And find thy home with me !
　　　　Birry—birr—wirr—burr—wurr !
　　　　　Cricket on a tree !
　　　　The man is wise 'neath sunny skies
　　　　　Who hums a song with thee !

JUMPING JANET.

REIN me now thy vagrant speed,
  My bright-eyed girl, my sprightly Janet!
I'll pen a rhyme for thee to read,
  Would these keen twinklers rest to scan it.
Thou art airy, light, elastic,
  Ever moving, never stopping,
With a squirrel's deft gymnastic,
  Ever springing, ever hopping.
'Tis well. Thou'rt nimble; so's a fly;
  But, for woman's proper training,
Jumping Janet must apply
  To her wits a little reining.
Nay, don't toss your head! 'tis fit,
  If the race you will be gaining,
That your dancing blood submit,
  Like the generous steed's, to training.

I am old and you are young,
　　My advice you should not scoff it ;
Use your ears, and not your tongue,
　　Janet, if you wish to profit.
Every morning when you rise,
　　That's my rule, my sprightly Janet,
What to do before you lies,
　　Clearly mark, and wisely plan it.
Every hour its business knows,
　　In a well-schemed day, my Janet,
Like a watch that surely goes,
　　Like a steady-wheeling planet.
Map your hours, and with the clock,
　　For the portioned work be ready ;
Like a limpet to a rock,
　　Cleaving to your purpose steady.
Work, as workmen work, indeed ;
　　Labour hard, and struggle stoutly,
With a wisely-tempered speed,
　　With an earnest heart devoutly.
Would you know the trick to charm
　　Pleasure from each seeming sorrow,
Grasp thy task with lusty arm,
　　Let the thing you do be thorough.

And when idle fancies come—
  Girlish heads are full of fancies—
Iridescent froth and scum,
  Bubble bright that gaily dances;
Thoughts of things that will be soon,
  Handsome men, and pretty faces,
Measured mountains in the moon,
  Ginghams, muslins, gimps, and laces;
Balls and concerts, promenades,
  Winter wear, and summer dresses,
Foppish youths, and prudish maids,
  Eagle eyes, and sable tresses;
Horrid murders, Church and State,
  Metaphysics, and cosmogony,
Granite slabs, and silver plate,
  Crimson curtains, old mahogany;
Strange elopements, foolish marriages,
  Melting tales of love romantic,
Sudden deaths, and sad miscarriages,
  Drownings in the deep Atlantic;
Stupid sermons, pious novels,
  Bruits of war among the nations,
Starving Celts in smoky hovels,
  Cumming on the Revelations:

Such vain thoughts a motley train,
  With a gaudy gay parading,
In a giddy-whirling brain,
  Find a place for masquerading.
Such, when they shall hover nigh,
  Though they twinkle ne'er so brightly,
Brush them from thee like a fly,
  Then buckle to thy work more tightly.
Ban the spirits with the spell
  Of a pious imprecation ;
Ev'n as Luther banned them well,
  When he worked at his translation.
Curb the whim, thy wit elastic
  To the work before thee chaining ;
Thou shalt know, by stern gymnastic,
  Thus the perfect woman's training.
Hour by hour, and day by day,
  If thou thus shalt wisely plan it ;
When your work is done, you may
  Sport with grace, my sprightly Janet !

STUDENT'S VACATION SONG.

Dear Thomas, I'm told
You're a student full bold,
And your looks the pale reader betray, my boy!
But I'm come now to call you,
Ere worse shall befall you,
To fling away books, and go play, my boy!

A dull, plodding youth,
A few grains of dry truth
May pick in this marrowless way, my boy!
But fresh feeling may never
Flow out, like a river,
From the parchment, so bloodless and grey, my boy!

Q

Think you the old bard,
You are spelling so hard,
Found his lusty, fresh song in this way, my boy?
O no! his blithe spirit
Strong joy did inherit
From life, like the bird in the May, my boy!

The truth must be told,
You'll soon lie 'neath the mould,
If you don't give your body fair play, my boy!
What boots all your yearning
For old Heathen learning,
When you're down, with the worms, 'neath the clay,
    my boy!

I've a house on the hill,
With a loch and a rill,
Where the troutlings still glancingly play, my boy!
Come with me to Yarrow
And fish away sorrow,
Through the length of the bright summer day, my
    boy!

THE WORKING MAN'S SONG.

I AM no gentleman, not I!
  No bowing, scraping thing!
I bear my head more free and high
  Than titled count or king.
I am no gentleman, not I!
  No, no, no!
And only to one Lord on high
  My head I bow.

I am no gentleman, not I!
  No vain and varnished thing!
And from my heart without a die,
  My honest thoughts I fling.

I am no gentleman, not I !
        No, no, no !
Our stout John Knox was none—and why
        Should I be so ?

I am no gentleman, not I !
    No mincing, modish thing !
In gay saloon a butterfly,
    Some wax-doll Miss to wing.
I am no gentleman, not I !
        No, no, no !
No moth, to sport in fashion's eye,
        A Bond Street beau !

I am no gentleman, not I !
    No bully, braggart thing !
With jockeys on the course to vie,
    With bull-dogs in the ring.
I am no gentleman, not I !
        No, no, no !
The working man might sooner die
        Than sink so low !

I am no gentleman, not I !
    No star-bedizened thing !

My fathers filched no dignity,
  By fawning to a king.
I am no gentleman, not I!
    No, no, no!
And to the wage of honesty
    My rank I owe!

I am no gentleman, not I!
  No bowing, scraping thing!
I bear my head more free and high
  Than titled count or king.
I am no gentleman, not I!
    No, no, no!
And thank the blessed God on high,
    Who made me so!

MAY SONG.

On Ettrick bank the primrose grows,
　Where the stream is winding clearly O !
Though the ash be grey, the birch is green,
　And the birds are chanting cheerly O !
Thou weary heart, why nurse the smart
　Of a fruitless grief so drearily ?
What should thee stay, to greet the May,
　Like a bird on the wing, so cheerily ?
　　　　Cuckoo, cuckoo, far in the wood !
　　　　　Sweet mavis on gowany lea !
　　　　O show me the trick of thy blithe May
　　　　　mood,
　　　　　And teach me to sing with thee !

Blow, softly, softly breezes blow !
  For the wound is rankling greenly yet !
And for him who is gone, whom I fear to name,
  The smart doth cut me keenly yet !
I laid him low, when in March the snow
  O'er the sod was drifting drearily,
And how shall I sing, like a bird on the wing,
  When the bright May sun shines cheerily ?
          Cuckoo, cuckoo, far in the wood !
          Sweet mavis on gowany lea !
          I love the sweet trick of thy blithe May
            mood,
          But grief still dwells with me !

APRIL SONG.

~~~~~~~~~

Hark! the birds are blithely hymning!
Leap, my heart! with glee be brimming!
Spring light-racing, dark days chasing,
  Comes—God bless thee, gentle Spring!

Though the ling'ring East be blowing,
I can scent the power of growing.
Where thou treadest, life thou spreadest;
  Bless thee, bless thee, gentle Spring!

Poplar sprouts, the hedge is green now,
Spiry larch in virgin sheen now,
~~~~~~~~~

Gently swinging to the singing
   Of sweet mavis, greets the Spring.

Pine upon the hoary mountain
Greets thy coming; foamy fountain,
With blithe bicker, quick and quicker,
   Ice-unshackled greets the Spring.

Violet blue, the green bank sprinkling,
Starry crow-flower golden twinkling,
Primrose clustered, thickly muster'd
   Wind-flowers weave a wreath for Spring!

Ha! my soul with songs is flooding!
Teem glad thoughts in eager budding!
Thou hast brought me wings to float me;
   Bless thee, bless thee, gentle Spring!

TO TORQUATUS.

(*From* HORACE.)

THAWED is the frost and the snow, the fields with
    green are fresh-coated,
        Green are the fresh-tufted trees ;
Earth is renewing her changes, the streams, with less-
    ening waters,
        Gently are gliding along.
Gaily the Graces come forth ; with the Nymphs in
    harmony twining,
        Deftly their dances they lead.
" HOPE IMMORTALITY NOT" the year declares, and
    the hour speaks,
        Rapidly driving the day.
Winter doth yield to the Spring, the Spring to
    Summer, the Summer

Yieldeth to Autumn ; and he,
When he hath scattered his fruitage, retreats ; and
   dreariest Winter
      Ruleth in dullness again.
Thus revolving it turns ;—the Moon repaireth her
   losses
      Speedily ; we, when we go
Down to the Shades with pious Æneas, rich Tullus,
   and Ancus,
      Dust and a shadow we are.
Who can tell if the gods the sum, which to-day we
   have numbered,
      Will with to-morrow increase ?
Greedily what thou hast left thy heir possesses ; but
   he, too,
      Quitteth how soon the bequest !
Once departed, when over thy head the merciless
   Minos
      Solemnly passes his doom,
Then, Torquatus, for thee shall birth, shall eloquence
   vainly,
      Vainly shall piety plead.
Vainly would Dian the chaste Hippolytus free from
   the darkness ;

Chastely he sleeps with the dead.
Theseus prevails not to break the bonds of Pirithous ;
Hades
Stronger him holdeth than Love.

THE GLENS OF NITHSDALE.

O THE bonnie, bonnie glens of Nithsdale,
  Where the clear rock-water flows,
Where the light birch nods its fragrant plumes,
  And the fair green breckan grows!
Glens, whose green folds were kind to hide
  The prophets of the hill,
Then when the shepherd's arm defied
  The monarch's godless will.
    O the bonnie, bonnie glens of Nithsdale,
    And O the bonnie green glens!

Soft o'er the hill I hear the note
  O' the peaceful, mild cuckoo!
Not now as then, when o'er the muir
  Came the trooper's harsh halloo,

Hunting the good and the godly men,
  Who preached the truth of God,
Splashing with murder the bonnie green glen,
  And drenching with blood the sod !
    O the bonnie, bonnie glens o' Nithsdale,
    And O the bonnie green glens !

O few are the houses that smoke on the hill,
  And the heirs of the godly are few !
How rare in the glen are the sons of the men
  Whose hand to their heart was true !
There's pride in a Duke, and there's pomp in a
    lord ;
  But the glory of brave Scottish men
Is the plaided cottar, who drew the sword
  For his faith, in the bonnie green glen !
    O the bonnie, bonnie glens o' Nithsdale,
    And O the bonnie green glens !

DREAMING DAVIE.

DAVIE was a quiet boy,
Hating every boisterous joy,
Slow of tongue, of temper slow,
Never first a stone to throw.
On the moor would sit alone,
Brooding on an old grey stone,
Or, wandering with a drooping head,
Pluck butterworts from oozy bed ;
 Surely there is something odd,
 All the people say, in Davie !
 Dreaming Davie ! dandering Davie !
 What's in Davie we shall see. .

Listless, sitting in the school
Master called him dreamy fool ;
Flies and spiders, buzzing gnats,
Rabbits, ferrets, newts, and bats,

Twittering swallows, cawing rooks,
All had charms for him but books ;
Greeks and Romans long since dead
Were never meant for Davie's head.
        Surely there is something odd,
        People say, about this Davie !
        Dreaming Davie ! dandering Davie !
        What's in Davie we shall see.

Davie's left the school—and lo !
Davie roaming now will go ;
Probes the nooks of every glen,
Scales the peaks of every Ben.
In the sunshine, in the shower,
Now a rock, and now a flower,
Peering round with knowing eyes,
Davie always finds a prize,
        Surely this is very odd,
        People say—Can this be Davie ?
        Once so dreaming, now so scheming,
        Full of teeming plans is he.

Davie now has wandered far,
In lands beneath the burning star,

Dredged the floor of every sea,
Where strange finny monsters be,
Crossed, by airy bamboo bridgè,
Clefts that part hoar Andes' ridge,
Scaled Mont Blanc, and tented high
On rosy snow, 'twixt Earth and sky.
  Surely this is very odd,
  People say—Can this be Davie?
  Daring Davie! dauntless Davie!
  Full of grand success is he.

In the list of men who know,
Europe now no name can show
Like to Davie's; Earth contains
Nought that's not in Davie's brains.
Prince Albert and the Queen, I'm told,
Hear Davie wisdom's stores unfold,
Though the master in the school
Called him little dreaming fool.
  Now men say, 'tis nothing odd
  He should have been a dreaming
   Davie!
  Well done, Davie! just so, Davie!
  Dreams beget great deeds, we see!

R

CONFESSION OF FAITH FOR ALL MEN.

WHAT a sinful son of Adam
  Should believe, and how,
In each heart 'tis graven, madam,
  Read, and know it now.
     'Tis a gospel old and new,
     Tongues and tribes attest it true ;
     And who denies this creed
     Is damned indeed !

Nothing comes from nothing truly ;
  God hath certainly
Wisely framed and ordered duly
  All the things you see.

Look and learn, vain babbling spare,
Trace the true, and love the fair;
And who denies this creed
Is damned indeed!

Satan rules the air; this wisely
Doctors teach to spell,
But here or there, or where precisely,
Satan himself may tell.
Crush the fiend that lurks within,
Hydra-headed monster Sin;
And who denies this creed
Is damned indeed!

Learning is not wisdom; fainly
Doctors will dispute,
But plies on plies the million vainly
Vamp a mouldy boot.
Woo the breeze, court sunny skies,
Like a tree thy thought will rise;
And who denies this creed
Is damned indeed!

Whoso scatters words with sorrows
Sows an eager land;

Wing thy speech like cunning arrows,
  Think with sword in hand.
      Watch and wait in quiet snare,
      Pluck, when it is ripe, the pear ;
      And who denies this creed
        Is damned indeed !

Know your ground and keep your footing,
  Battle not with air ;
When you know what thing you're shooting,
  Bravely do and dare.
      Turn the screw and drive the wedge,
      Every step the next will pledge ;
      And who denies this creed
        Is damned indeed !

When you fall, remain not lying,
  Luck has many ways ;
Urge the hour, the chance be plying,
  Death is in delays.
      So Napoleon warred and won,
      By strong will earth's topmost son ;
      And who denies this creed
        Is damned indeed !

Greet the Devil when you fairly
 Meet him in the face !
Scan him coolly o'er, and yarely
 He will run and race.
   Should he buckle for the fight,
   Beat him quite, or die outright ;
   Whoso believes this creed
    Is saved indeed !

BOOK V.

CAMENA.

"*At enim Latine scribendorum carminum, meâ quidem sententiâ, neque omnibus prohibendus est mos, neque omnibus commendandus. Hoc vero certissimum habéo, neminem de Romanorum literis bene omnino meritum esse, aut œque judicare posse, nisi qui sedulo ac diligenter tunc oratoribus tunc poetis juvenis incubuerit, strenue autem atque enixe in eisdem vir sese exercuerit.*" LANDOR.

Wer fremde Sprachen nicht kennt weiss nichts von seiner eigenen.
GOETHE.

IN JANUM.

Hymnus Kalendis Januariis cantandus.

JANE, volventum caput atque custos
Mensium, certi bone rector anni,
Janitor coeli, tua dum sonamus
    Festa, faveto!

Mixta pugnabant elementa rerum
Ima supremis, piceamque noctem
Intererrabant sine lege raræ
    Semina lucis.

Mole confusa Chaos occupabat
Cuncta; dum portas reserare coeli
Claviger doctus daret ordinati
    Munera Solis.

Tum dies nigram variare noctem,
Incipit, certos celerare cursus
Astra, tum Phœbe reparare menses,
    Te duce, Jane.

Leniter vastâ polus incitari
Mole, quâ vultu gemino vigil tu
Igneâ celsus specularis arce
    Omnia circum.

Dux et annosi moderator ævi,
Tu pedum gressus sapiens meorum
Dirigas, firmes; trepidum levemque
    Tu stabilito!

Heu! quot et quantis, vaga gens, procellis
(Triste!) mortales ferimur, quibus nec
Carceres certi, neque certa fixa est
    Meta viarum.

Per nefas præceps furiosa turba
More cæcorum ruit in barathrum,
Dum voret lassos laceretque dirâ
    Fauce Charybdis.

Me bifrons Jani quoties imago
Adspicit, pictâ moneat loquelâ,
" Ore propenso properare perge ; at
    Respice retro."

AMORIS PHILOSOPHIA.

Vivida cur rumpant nigrantes fulmina nubes
  Dic mihi ; dic terram cur properata petant ;
Alliciat rigidum cur vis magnetica ferrum,
  Axem cur gelidum nautica quærat acus.
Segnia cur trahat electrum corpuscula frictum,
  Ignis et illiso cur silice exsiliat :
Dic mihi, si sapias, quid sit vis chymica : quæ vis
  Quæ modo pugnabant nunc elementa liget.
Mystica cur agitent atomos connubia ; durus
  Cur lapidem miro tangat amore lapis.
Cur montis nutet sublimis vertice pinus,
  Irriguæ vallis cur sit amica salix ;
Cur hodie summos moveant vix flamina ramos,
  Quæ valeant totum sternere sæpe nemus.

Dic mihi Christicolam cur te lux norit et Anglum,
    Cur non Paganum Graiugenamque virum.
Cur tibi nunc facili vegetæ conamine vitæ
    Cor micet, exsanguem crastina fata premant;
Hæc mihi dic sapiens; sapienti tunc ego dicam
    Cur de tot pulchris pulchra sit una mihi.

PRECES NOCTURNÆ.

TEMPORE nocturno, per sancta silentia cœli
    Te votis veneror, te prece, summe Deus!
Jam me non fremitus, non dissona turba fatigat
    Stultorum, rauci non fera verba fori.
Jam lassata auris lenimina debita poscit,
    Curarum requiem pectora lassa petunt.
Omnia jam velant placidæ solamina noctis,
    Omnibus alta quies, dulcis ubique sopor;
Qualiter et dea per terræ non turbida turbas,
    Procedit tacito candida Luna polo.
O utinam quæ tecta hominum, quæ corpora lassa
    Hæc eadem teneat consona corda quies!
O utinam pleno descendat numine præsens,
    Mulceat et sancto pectus amore Deus!

Sidera contemplor, miris quam cursibus illa
  Incipiant longas perficiantque vias!
Nulla mora est illis ; placida sed lege feruntur,
  Nec cessare viâ, nec trepidare queunt.
Nos tamen incerti gressu titubante vagamur
  Et vagulæ tremulos spesque metusque tenent ;
Et nunc correpti quasi febre impellimur ; et nunc
  Sternimus in pigro languida membra toro.
Summe Deus, dubiæ per turbida compita vitæ,
  Dirige tu gressus, tu moderare, meos !
Ah ! non humanæ pollent exquirere vires
  Ad vitam humanam quæ sibi poscit homo.
Tu mihi, queis careo, blandi modulamina cordis
  Concedas, gratum desque tenere modum ;
His contentus ero ; sint hæc mihi vota peracta,
  Sit studiosa quies, sit sine lite labor !

EST DEUS IN NOBIS.

Omnia declarant tua numina, summe Creator,
  Per mare, per terras, fulget ubique Deus.
Sidera divini vultus stant lumina; flores
  Exsiliunt, vivo quâ volat ille pede.
Spectanti deerit finis miracula rerum
  Tanta, per innumeras tam variata vices.
Sed tu, si sapias, oculis fræna injice : major
  Regnat in augusto pectore, crede, Deus.
Intus alit sanctâ Dominus præcordia flammâ;
  Tu ne sit flammæ frigida cura cave.
Hic tibi fons vitæ, tibi sol, tibi sidera ; cuncta
  Quæ tua teque vocas pectora parva tenent.
Injice fræna oculis ; nimio fluitantia luxu
  Subsidant proprio lumina fida loco.

Heu ! dum scrutaris nullo moderamine vastas,
    Longinquas, varias, res sine fine vagas,
Excidis ipse tibi ; metiris sidera, soles ;
    Languescit vitæ fax tibi sacra tuæ.
Omnes descripto procedunt tramite ; tu quid
    Omnia nosse vorax, sed nihil esse velis ?
Heu miser ! in proprium sapiens te conde sacellum !
    Fontem nosse vacet, quâ tua vita latet !
Omnia plena Dei ; ter sancto jure timendum
    Includunt magnum pectora fida Deum.

DEO OPTIMO MAXIMO.

(Gratiarum actio Kalendis Januariis.)

TURBIDUS nimbis, tumidus procellis
Volvitur mensis, gelidus novorum
Mensium ductor, tua, Jane, prisca
    Nomina monstrans.

Heu! quibus grando crepitans fenestras
Verberat plagis, niviumque quanti
Turbines proflant Hiemis globatas
    Naribus iras!

At mihi ridet foculus furenti
Tutus a flatu, placet otioso
Dulce Museum, micat et nitentum
    Theca librorum.

Quæ dapes ! nunc me VENUSINUS æquâ
Sobrius Musâ rapuit, rapit nunc
Vortice excitas agitans Camœnas
    STATIUS ultro ;

Sive me mulcet facilis fluenti
Garrulus venâ, trepidantis instar
Rivuli, NASO, sapiens canoras
    Texere nugas ;

Sive Titanum revocavit ingens
ÆSCHYLUS pugnas, stetit et deorum
Par minis, victor sine vi virili
    Mente Prometheus ;

Sive cœlestis stimulavit aures
Buccinæ clangor, quoties superbâ
Mente MILTONUS placet, et severæ
    Gloria frontis.

Tu, Deus, tantas bonus et benignus
Copias fundis, comites parasti
Tot mihi doctos ; tua tot quietus
    Prata totondi.

Tu mihi parci, bone, des, Creator,
Compotem voti placidamque mentem ;
Sic focos tutos tenuesque mensas
Fidus amabo.

TU MIHI ADES.

Tu mihi semper ades ; primâ quum luce diei
   Ædibus in summis parva fenestra micat,
Sub trabe quâ notâ nidum suspendit hirundo,
   Garrula quæ querulos fundit ab ore sonos,
Tu mihi ades ; nullo non tempore grata puella,
   Noctes atque dies tu mihi semper ades.

Tu mihi ades, medio quum Phœbus volvitur axe,
   Quum trepidat rapidis fervida vita rotis,
Quum fera turba hominum clamosis compita complet
   Vocibus, et rixis perstrepit omne forum.
Sed tu sola sonas adstans mihi, grata puella :
   Auribus atque oculis una ades usque meis.

Tu mihi ades, properans condit quum lumina Phœbus,
    Vesper et occiduo leniter axe rubet;
Tum duri cessant hominumque boumque labores,
    Et nemore in fusco turba canora silet;
Sed non cessat amor; dulcis tua perstat imago,
    Ut veniente die, sic fugiente, mihi.

Tu mihi ades tacito cum surgunt sidera ponto,
    Seque pruinosâ Nox nigra veste tegit;
Languida tum longos producunt corpora somnos,
    Sollicitudinibus cordaque cæca vacant;
Omnia muta manent, placidæque simillima morti,
    Sed mihi vivit amor; tu mihi semper ades.

LUTHERI HYMNUS.

(Eine feste Burg ist unser Gott.)

<div style="text-align: center">~~~~~~~~~~</div>

ARX est, arx et aënea
Turris ; præsidium stat Deus et salus
Nobis ; robore præpotens
Nos urgente malo fortiter expedit.
Nam priscus cacodæmon
Jam non segnis adest, jam properat minax !
Cincto viribus et dolis
Huic non terra parem, non similem tenet.

Nobis non hominum fides ;
Sic sic pernicies et cita mors foret !
Nobis arma Sionia
Nobis dux superis missus ab arcibus.

Quisnam est ? quis mihi nomina
Dicat ? Christus, io ! filius ést Dei !
Nobis hic Deus unus est,
Hic, hic fertur eques victor in omnia !

Quid si terra draconibus,
Quid si dæmoniis Orcus hiet feris ?
Sed nos non timor occupat,
Nos felix, duce te, meta manet mali.
Qui latum regit aëra
In nos cassa parat retia subdolus ;
Damnavit Deus improbum ;
Vox, vox, parvula vox dæmona dejicit !

Nam verbum Domini sacrum
Non istis digitis tangere fas erit ;
Jam, jam, numen adest Dei ;
Vincendi Domino curriculum patet !
Nobis diripiant domos,
Uxores jugulent, caraque pignora,
Vitæque insidias struant !
Frustra ; veridici verba manent Dei.

MUSA TEUTONICA.

NON te potentum limina principum
Germana blandis Musa caloribus
  Fovere parvam, non superbus
Te dubiam, titubante nisu,

Rexit patronus. Maximus a suis
Aversus, (eheu !), nec proprio grege
  Stipatus exturbavit ultro
Te patriâ Fredericus, aulâ.

At tu recentis plena Dei, fovens
Non deprimendam mente superbiam,
  Nullisque sustentata fulcris,
Spernis humum, nebulasque findis.

Et nunc, volatu liberior vago,
Cœlum pererras haud solitis viis,
    Cunctas ut Europe per urbes
Intrepidam stupeat Camenam.

ELEGI GOETHIANI.

EDITE saxa sonos! stellis contermina templa
    Dicite! quid cessas, mutaque, Musa, manes?
Vivis adhuc certe; spirant sacra mœnia vitam,
    Urbs æterna; mihi cur tua saxa silent?
Limina quis monstret, caræ quis tecta puellæ,
    Quæ mea consumens recreet ossa simul?
Prævideo nondum properæ vestigia plantæ,
    Quasque petam notas, quas repetamque vias?
Auguror et nondum non desidis otia vitæ,
    Damnaque congestis quam potiora lucris?
Hospes adhuc prudens delubra, palatia, lustro,
    Et scrutor prisci rudera rara fori.
Sed mox hæc cessent; tua tunc ante omnia templa
    Excipient cultum vatis amantis, Amor.

Mundus inest Romæ—fateor—sed, amore remoto,
    Non mundus mundus, Romave Roma foret.

Græcia sarcophagos vitâ decorabat et urnas ;
    Exercet varios Baccha proterva choros,
Cum Satyris ; buccas inflat sibi capripedum grex,
    Rumpit et infrænos buccina rauca sonos.
Tympana tunduntur ; tinnitus æra repulsa
    Ingeminant : credas marmora dura loqui.
Aliferæ volucres baccas de palmite carpunt,
    Nec turbant dulces murmura rauca dapes.
Nec turbatur Amor ; magno sed murmure laetus
    In variâ turbâ ventilat ille faces.
Copia sic vitæ mortem tegit ; et quasi vitam
    Exiguâ gustant ossa quieta domo.
Sic vitâ cassum viridem spirantia vitam
    Olim me vatem carmina sacra tegant !

EPIGRAMMATA SCHILLERIANA.

DE ILIADE ET WOLFII ASSECLIS.

ILIADOS patres fuerint quot, cum sit Homerus
    Nullus, Germani garrula bella movent ;
Sed mater tamen una manet, certissima matris
    NATURÆ proles lineamenta refert.

IN QUEMDAM QUI HOMINES AD SUAM NORMAM
REFINGERE NITEBATUR.

" Omnia tentavi pravi medicamina mundi,
    At nisi livores præmia nulla tuli !"
Scire velis, bone, quanta hominum grex debeat esse
    Cura tibi ?—dicam ; fallere Musa nequit.
Sit tibi magna fides hominum, sit maxima semper,
    Quem factis reddas dent tibi corda typum ;
Si quemque offendas angusto in tramite vitæ,
    Huic tendas sociam, si velit ipse, manum ;

Sed rorem et pluvias, pravi et medicamina mundi,
  Hæc bona curabunt numina cras, ut heri.

PINGENDI REGULA.

Si mundi captare velis et vota piorum,
  Pinge voluptates, pinge sed et Satanam.

CONFESSIO FIDEI.

Quæ te religio tenet e tot millibus?—at me
  Nulla tenet—Quare?—religione vetor.

ULYSSES.

Vastas tentat aquas, patriam visurus, Ulysses,
  Quâ Scylla et dirâ fauce Charybdis hiat.
Per mala dura maris, mala per durissima terræ,
  Jactatus, Stygium fertur ad usque Jovem.
Tandem Ithacæ somno victus subit ostia; somno
  Surgit, et est patriæ nescius ipse suæ!

JUPITER HERCULEM ADLOQUITUR.

Non mea fecerunt te nectare pocula divum,
  Sed divina tulit vis tibi vina Jovis.

COLUMBUS.

Finde salum, bone dux! quid si risusve sequatur,
  Desperetve viam rector et ipse ratis,
Hesperias preme tu partes; latet ora refulgens
  Partibus Hesperiis; jam tibi, jamque patet!
Fide Deo (Deus est nobis in pectore); quod si
  Non sit, debetur sed tamen ora tibi.
Mystica lex mentemque hominis mundumque ligavit;
  Præmonstrant veras pectora vera vias.

MAJESTAS POPULI.

Majestas populi! vulgus non sperno; sed eheu!
  Paucorum sophiæ gloria rara fuit.
Victrices paucæ, sortes ducuntur inanes
  Multæ; congesto pulvere gemma latet.

ARTIFEX DICENDI.

Ostentant omnes opera artifices sine culpa;
  Verbis qui pollet multa poeta tacet.

IDEM ALITER.

Divitias promunt alii monstrantque magistri;
  Is bonus est scriptor qui bene celat opes.

SAPIENTIA ET PRUDENTIA.

Palladis æthereæ sublimia templa petentem
　　Non derisorum detinuere joci.
Proxima lippa videt Prudentia littora; non quâ
　　Per maria alta micat fulgida meta sopho.

VERI PRÆDICATIO.

Tu cave ne veri emittas oracula plebi;
　　Mittentis repetent heu! tua tela caput.

MARTINI TABERNA.

Quisquis ades properans, paullisper siste viator,
    Quâ tibi Martini clara taberna patet.
Quisquis eris, capitis cui sint velamina grata,
    Intres; Martini bella taberna patet.
Quisquis amas pandos petasos, celsosque galeros,
    En tibi Martini nota taberna vacat.
Me populus laudat, popularis merx mihi prostat,
    Vix tantum plebis parva taberna capit.
Non mea constringit vexatam fabrica frontem,
    Non cedit vento fabrica laxa nimis.
Non mea tabescunt pluviâ, nive, rore, procellis,
    Grandinibus firmâ fabrica facta manu.
Omnibus est vitium mortalibus : at sine labe
    Martini docta fabrica facta manu.

T

Destituet cassis fortes, Papamque tiaras,
　　Sublimes apices fulmina prima petunt;
Sed tuto incedit velamine, si cui rarum
　　Martini petasum rara taberna dedit!

VERSICULI SATURNALES.

Quid facis exiguis latitans, Hornelle, latebris ?
    Artocreas libat gnaviter ille sacrum.
Inserto magnum promens sibi pollice prunum,
    "Quam puer egregius" clamitat "ecce fui !"

Euge ! sophos ! fidicen felis ! quam bestia bella !
    Euge ! super lunæ cornua vacca salit.
Nescio quâ catulus ridet dulcedine ludi,
    Insequitur cursu lanx cochleare novo !

Quo tua te properum vestigia devia ducunt
    Anser ?—eho ! nullâ lege vagatur avis.
Fertur et in scalas anserculus ! improbe, quid nunc !
    Heu thalamum dominæ scandit ad usque meæ !

HERBARUM METAMORPHOSIS.

(*Ad exemplar poematis Goethiani*)

TE turbant, varii flores, te, vita, colores,
    Confundit picti copia multa soli?
Et, cum raucarum procedant agmina vocum,
    Nomina sed trudunt nomina rauca tamen.
Omnibus est species diversa, sed omnibus una est,
    Mystica lex flores sacraque norma regit.
Sit mihi, quam cupio, felix facundia linguæ,
    Arcanum ut possim pandere, vita, tibi.
Adspicias tenuis quam gestiat herba vigescens
    E teneris teneros elicuisse gradus.
Seminis e grano surgit, simul augmina lenta
    Prompserit e gravido gleba benigna sinu,
Mobilis ut tangat blanda irritamina lucis
    Frons tenera, inveniat lætificumque jubar.

Res simplex semen ; perfectæ sed tamen herbæ,
  Intus erat species, implicitusque typus ;
Frons, radix, germenque latent in semine parvo,
  Sed vaga forma tamen, sed color omnis abest.
Corticibus duris sic herba tenella tenetur,
  In sicco grano vita quieta sedet ;
Donec lene madens turgescat semen, et ultro
  Emicet e densa nocte, petatque diem ;
Sed simplex herbæ nascens manet usque figura,
  Sic puer est simplex, si quis adultus erit.
Jam culmum nova vis effert ; mox augmine nodi
  Excipiunt nodos, et loca celsa petunt ;
Sed simili semper formâ, variâ sed eâdem,
  Herba viget, primum pandere læta typum.
Jamque unâ frondes variantur imagine ; jamque
  E glomere exserti per spatia ampla patent ;
Pluribus et sectis iteratur partibus herba,
  Et frons in frondes finditur usque novas.
Sic amat in vastos arbor se pandere ramos
  Et multis (mirum !) luxuriare modis.
Naturam credas nullos sibi ponere fines,
  Ubere tam pleno magnificoque tumet.
Sed hic grata sibi sapiens moderamina figit,
  Et gradibus lentis egregiora petit ;

Jam magis et placido tenuantur sanguine venæ,
   Jam tenuata viget tota figura magis.
Surgit dein gracilis sine fronde pedunculus; et mox
   Mirantem floris fabrica mira capit.
Nam petala in pulchrum vis vivida digerit orbem,
   Plurima, quæ numeres, quæ numeroque carent;
Cumque calix presso refugus se solverit axe,
   Panditur in plenum picta corona diem.
Sic splendet demum summo Natura triumpho
   Et gradibus cumulat leniter apta gradus;
Ut stupeas, iterumque novus stupor occupet ossa,
   Flos quoties summâ pendulus arce tremit.
Sed non usque manet prænuntia gloria floris;
   Quin genetrice dei tangitur ille manu,
Contrahiturque citus; tenui jam stamina filo
   Verticibus flexis fœdera sancta petunt;
Et jam cum pare par dulces irritat amores,
   Circumstatque aras fervida turba sacras;
Ipse Hymenæus adest, gratique feruntur odores,
   Sparsaque vitali pulvere fila rubent.
Jam se disjungunt; et germina singula turgent,
   Quæ tenero in gremio mollia poma tegunt.
Et hic vivificum genetrix vis conficit orbem,
   Excipit at sollers vincula rupta manus;

Scilicet ut longo producta propagine vivant
  Corpore cum toto singula membra simul.
Adspice nunc varios flores, nunc, vita, colores,
  Te turbat picti copia nulla soli;
Mystica nunc reserata patet lex sacraque norma,
  Clamat et ex herbis vox manifesta Dei.
Ast hic si pateat sacri tibi litera libri,
  Mutata specie, linea nota manet;
Sive eruca trahat larvam, seu papilionis
  Ala micet, vultus seu sibi mutet homo.
Sic nosterque accrevit amor; cognoscere vultus
  Fons erat; e dulci dulcior usus erat;
Vis et amicitiæ dein vinxit pectora; donec
  Protulit et flores, pomaque firmus amor.
Hæc reputa; reputa blandi solamina amoris
  Quot fuerint nobis, quam variata Venus.
Præsentemque diem liba; sit et una voluntas
  Nobis—hic fructus summus amoris erit—
Unaque mens, ut quos dulcis concordia junxit
  Cum pare par læti regna serena petant.

NOTES.

NOTES.

Note 1, p. 3.—Patrick Hamilton, the first of the more notable martyrs of the Scottish Reformation, was born in the year 1504, and suffered martyrdom at St Andrews in the year 1528. See Knox's History of the Reformation, vol. i. p. 13 ; Laing ; and Lorimer's Life of the martyr, 1857,—a valuable little work.

Note 2, p. 6.—The brutal and unfeeling martyrdom of Margaret Wilson and Margaret M'Lauchlan on the eleventh of May 1685 will remain for ever in the minds of the Scottish people, as a memorial of that perverse and pig-headed generation of crowned formalists, who employed themselves for more than a century in forcing Episcopacy upon a people essentially Presbyterian. See Macaulay, ch. iv. I have followed Wodrow.

Note 3, p. 10.—James Renwick, the last of the noble Scottish band of protesters for liberty of conscience, suffered martyrdom in the Grassmarket of Edinburgh in the month of February 1688. This pure-minded, generous, and intrepid youth, of whom the then world of hirelings and time-servers was not worthy, publicly declared and subscribed the great principle of the Revolution of 1688, at a time when the majority of the best public men of that day were only beginning to dream of its possibility. Eternal honour to his name, the brave, the heroic, the unsullied ! When our petty squabbles of Church politics shall have passed away from the hearing of Time, as a shallow din of tinkling cymbals, the name

of Renwick shall live in the thoughts of the philosophical historian,
as one of the greatest of the great.

<blockquote>
" Strongest minds
Are often those of whom the noisy world
Hears least."
</blockquote>

Renwick was born in Glencairn, Dumfriesshire, near the beautiful
little village of Minnyhive, where a neat little monument has recently been erected to his memory.

Note 4, p. 15.—The churchyard of Wigton is beautifully situated on a rising ground overlooking the lovely bay of Wigton.
Immediately south of the town the river Bladnoch flows into the
bay, at the mouth of which the two Margarets were drowned by
the brutal dragoons of James II. The inscription on the tombs of
the martyrs still exhibits the old inscription in characters particularly fresh and clear. On a rising ground behind the town an
obelisk has very recently been erected in memory of the martyr
maidens.

Note 5, p. 18.—See Knox's History, vol. i. p. 173, whom I have
closely followed. The deed celebrated in the text took place in
the year 1546. That it was not a murder in the criminal sense of
the word, but a just retribution for wicked deeds, besides being
politically a wise act, no impartial thinker can doubt. Beaton
was a man who intruded into the Church of Christ, as his greatest
admirers admit, from purely ambitious and worldly motives; and
being seated in the seat of the Holiest, this godless and cruel
man used his unsanctified power for the purpose of persecuting
and annihilating the only men then existing who were faithfully
preaching the truth of God in this land. In the eye of Heaven,
Beaton was a traitor and a murderer. He murdered Wishart;
and if he was murdered himself afterwards, he had no more
right to complain than any other mortal who has been made to
feel the eternal justice of that text, " *Whoso sheddeth man's blood,
by man shall his blood be shed.*" The talk about LAW and LE-
GITIMATE AUTHORITY in such cases may amuse the shallow and
console the coward; but it has no meaning to the consistent
thinker. Those who talk with a pious horror of assassination
ought to bear in mind, that when wolves in sheep's clothing exer-
cise open force over the sheep, there is nothing for the faithful
shepherd but to use secret force, when opportunity offers. The

magistrate has no right to bear the sword in support of injustice ;
nor do Cardinals enjoy any sacred privilege to dye their stockings
purple in the blood of just men.   As to the policy of the act there
can be no doubt.   Beaton was the most talented and the most
energetic captain of injustice and advocate of lies in those days ;
and his death gave the Reformation room to breathe and to grow,
which otherwise might have been crushed under the squelch of his
ruthless foot.

NOTE 6, p. 21.—With regard to Myln, our last Protestant martyr, who suffered in the month of April 1558, I have followed the
account from Fox, as it is given in the Appendix to Laing's edition
of Knox.   Vol. i. p. 550.

NOTE 7, p. 33.—I recommend all persons who visit Abbotsford
and Melrose to go on to Selkirk, from whence a pleasant pastoral
walk of some twenty miles will take them up to the mountain
church of Ettrick, where the famous theologian THOMAS BOSTON
lies buried.   The scenery is full of green, quiet beauty, of a character very similar to the lovely vale of Newlands, between Buttermere
and Derwentwater, in the Lake country.

NOTE 8, p. 36.—I took this story from *Simpson's Traditions of
the Covenanters*, a well-known book, which, notwithstanding some
faults of literary execution, gives the reader, by mere accumulation
of similar cases, a more vivid idea of the bloody times of tyrannous
Episcopacy in Scotland than the most elegant pages of Macaulay.
The farm of Dalquhairn is beautifully situated in the mountain solitude, on the hill road between Sanquhar and Carsphairn.
The whole of that country is sacred to the memory of our brave
peasants, the untitled heroes of

" times
Whose echo rings in Scotland to this hour."

Happy the man who can drink the breezy mountain air in these
green solitudes, and seek for no other company than the memory
of these plaided protesters !

NOTE 9, p. 41.—The title of this song suggests to me the pro-
priety of stating, in a few short sentences, the grounds on which,
as a philosophical student of history—for no one will suspect me of
partizanship—I am convinced that the Covenanters, who have been

so liberally abused by all sorts of fashionable writers, are the only true heroes of the Scottish history of the seventeenth century; and that all attempts to put the Cavaliers in their place must issue in ridiculous discomfiture.

(1.) It is quite certain, according to the New Testament and the practice of the first centuries, that the Church of Christ does not mean the clerical order, but it means emphatically and prominently the Christian people, the assembly, the congregation, the body of the faithful.

(2.) The Christian people, as such, have an inherent, divine, and inalienable right to act in religious matters according to the free verdict of their conscience, and not to be coerced into creeds or forms of worship by any extrinsic power, clerical or secular.

(3.) Any distinct association of human beings, composing what we call a nation, and professing Christianity, is entitled to follow the conscience of the majority in making a national confession of faith, and to resist dictation in this matter, whether from priests or politicians, who, in so far as they attempt to debauch the free national conscience, are usurpers, and ought to be cast down.

(4.) The Scottish people did, by many very manifest and indubitable acts, declare and profess their faith in Presbytery as the most scriptural form of church government, according to the best of their insight; and this their declaration was formally confirmed by the Act of Parliament 1560.

(5.) Notwithstanding this public and constitutional declaration, King James VI., Kings Charles I. and II., and James II., did, in a most false and treacherous way, form a conspiracy to rob the Scottish people of this their freely chosen faith; and did, during a period of more than one hundred years, proceed to the execution of this conspiracy in a series of public acts, characterised by falsehood, fraud, force, and cruelty of the most atrocious description.

(6.) That for these acts resistance to the government of these kings, so far from being criminal, was to be regarded as the highest heroism; and to the men who practised this heroism, in days of gross selfishness and cowardice, the Scottish people owe their independence, and all that is manly and worthy of admiration in their character.

(7.) The Scottish Cavaliers, whatever might have been the personal virtues of some of them, or the brilliant qualities of others, were, as a body, engaged in the cause of falsehood, injustice, tyranny, and oppression, and therefore are justly regarded by all true Scotsmen with hatred, and by all philosophical thinkers with pity or contempt.

(8.) The principles for which the Covenanters fought and bled, are the very principles which were established by the Revolution of 1688, and which lie at the bottom of the whole political constitution and social philosophy of Britain at the present hour.

(9.) Any offensive peculiarities of doctrine or manners exhibited by individual Presbyterians, are no more to be made a ground of reproach against the whole body, than the licentiousness and corruption of the Court of Charles II. are to be set down to the account of the whole body of the Cavaliers who supported him.

(10.) Those who are fond to object to the Covenanters that they were intolerant, ought to bear in mind that toleration in matters of state-religion is an innovation only of yesterday, unknown alike to Plato, the greatest philosopher of ancient times, and to Calvin, one of the greatest theologians of modern times. Besides, toleration, which is a very pretty phrase in times of peace, can have no meaning in times of war. Soldiers do not tolerate one another; they cut one another's throats. So, in times of religious warfare, there can be no toleration, so long as the struggle lasts. We are learning to tolerate Popery only now; and even now not altogether. If the Covenanters were intolerant in those days of a life and death struggle, so were the Episcopalians; only the Covenanters, so long as they remained on Scottish ground, were in the right, and the Episcopalians in the wrong. If a man uses violence in word or deed, it is by no means a matter of indifference of what cause he is the champion, and whether he stands in a defensive or an aggressive position. To be over-zealous in a good cause may often be pardonable; while even a little zeal in the service of falsehood, fraud, and force, is a great sin.

NOTE 10, p. 44.—In this ballad I have followed very closely the account given by our genial Reformer in his History, vol. i. p. 260, Laing. The word *marmoset*, signifying a sort of monkey, is applied by Knox to the idol. I put it into the mouth of the mob.

NOTE 11, p. 49.—See CHAMBERS' *Annals of Scotland*, vol. ii. p. 103, year and date as in the text. The learned author says, on the authority of Wodrow, that the name of this mettlesome dame was not GEDDES, but MEAN. But, however this be, Fame has baptized her into Geddes, and with that appellation she must live through the ages, and will be famous as long as Scotland and Scotsmen are remembered.

NOTE 11, p. 82.—The wood-sorrel, *oxalis acetosella*, very abundant in our Scottish woods. From this plant oxalic acid is extracted.

NOTE 12, p. 86.—By the liberality for which the Free Church is so famous, very few of these cottage vicarages are now to be seen; but the verses in the text refer to a period shortly after the Disruption, when Free Church manses were not known.

NOTE 13, p. 88.—The farm of Ellisland, occupied by Burns before he took up the gauger trade, lies on the west bank of the Nith, about six miles north of Dumfries. The whole country is passing beautiful, and well worthy of more frequent visits than it receives from our English tourists. To them, also, I recommend a trip into the neighbouring counties of Kirkcudbright and Wigton, districts full of unfrequented and unsuspected beauty.

NOTE 14, p. 91.—The Lurlei-rock, on the Rhine above Boppart, is well known to tourists. I took the materials of the legend from SCHREIBER's *Handbuch fur Reisende am Rhein*, an old guide-book. Henry Heine's song on the same subject is well known.

NOTE 15, p. 122.—I owe an apology to the English reader for the appearance of this German hymn in a book of English poems. The fact is, the composition is dear to me, as the memorial of a time when I lived more in the German than in the English world, and when German words came gushing out of my full heart as naturally as if I had been born on the banks of the Rhine. I have also a conviction, now when I reflect on the matter, that the German is, of all languages, the best fitted for expressing, with grace and significance, such ideas as those that found vent in the present effusion.

NOTE 16, p. 190.—This famous lyric stands single, within the compass of my reading, as a composition combining a great philosophical principle and accuracy of scientific detail with the highest poetical beauty. The measure of the original is elegiac; for which I agree with Bulwer (see his translations from Schiller) that our ballad measure of fourteen syllables is the best substitute. On Goethe's botanical philosophy, generally, the reader will consult the poet's Life, by Lewis, a work which will be long remembered as one of the great biographical masterpieces of the present age. My admiration of this poem of Goethe is so great, that I was induced to try another version of it in Latin, which the reader will find at the end of the present volume.

NOTE 17, p. 214.—The hero of this little descriptive song is Sir Andrew Halliday, a native of Annandale, to the poetical aspect of whose character I was introduced by Dr Carlyle, when hospitably entertained by him in his snug little cell near Ecclefechan. About Sir Andrew's youth, see particularly "Poems by JOHN JOHNSTONE, Edinburgh, 1857 ;" a little work containing some interesting notices of Scottish peasant life, in the latter half of the last century.

NOTE 18, p. 224.—With regard to the evils of the one-sided large farm system, and the wholesale expatriation of the Highlanders, I have seen no reason to change the opinions expressed by me in the Notes to my *Lays and Legends*, p. 360. The articles on this subject which appeared in the *Edinburgh Review* and elsewhere, merely played dexterously with the accidents of the question, and left the essence untouched. The impolicy of the large farm system is admitted by a late practical writer, "MACKAY on the Management of Landed Property in the Highlands of Scotland. Blackwood, 1858."

NOTE 19, p. 229.—The bird here referred to is one of the Caprimulgus or goatsucker tribe, well known to naturalists.

NOTE 20, p. 234.—The cricket on the tree is the Latin *Cicada*, Italian *Cicala*, and the old Greek τιττιξ. I heard it whirring away most musically in a very hot day in June, as I was wending up from the plain of Marathon, by the hill road, across to the Cephissus. It will be observed that all Greek words in κός—shortened into κό by the modern Greeks—have the full accent on the last syllable, like our word *engineer;* though the Oxonians, perversely pronounce such words with the Latin accent on the antepenult.

THE END.

U